Trouble at the Circle Cross

Trouble at the Circle Cross

Ted Beltz

This book is dedicated to Diane Beltz: my partner, mentor, spiritual advisor, wife of over forty years, mother of my children, and the one I love more than life itself.

Trouble at the Circle Cross
Copyright © 2014 by Ted Beltz

All rights reserved. Except for brief quotations in printed reviews, no portion of this publication may be reproduced in any form or by any means without the prior permission of the author. Printed in the United States of America.

This book is a work of fiction. Any references to historical events, real people, or real places are used fictitiously. Other names, characters, places, and events are products of the author's imagination. Any resemblance to actual events, places, or persons, living or dead, is entirely coincidental.

Design, editing, and production: Steve Lewis
Cover artwork: *"Coyote Crossing"*
  Courtesy of Duward Campbell. Used by Permission.
Chapter inset image: *"Ropin' a Stray"* by Justsin Wells.
  Courtesy of Stephen Zimmer, Double Z Bar Ranch,
  Cimarron, New Mexico. Used by Permission.

Library of Congress Control Number: 2014946462
ISBN: 978-0-9892807-6-1

 Published by Eagle Trail Press PO Box 3671 Parker, Colorado 80134 info@EagleTrailPress.com

A solitary horseback rider worked his way along the sloping side of a deep, rough canyon. Huge boulders and dead trees littered the bottom, accumulated there after some long-ago flood. The rider was following a faint game trail made over many years. His name was Doug Jepsen—ol' Slim, his horse, and BC his Border Collie made up the rest of the group. Doug was looking for signs of a grizzly, because he had seen unmistakable tracks in the mud by a dirt tank about two hundred yards back where this canyon emptied into a large grassy swale. By the direction of the prints at the tank, it seemed the bear was headed up this canyon.

Suddenly Slim's head came up, ears pointed, nostrils flared, straining to detect some scent on the breeze. Doug was raking the canyon with his eyes to determine what the horse was scenting. BC also sensed something and was sniffing the air. Doug couldn't see anything, but eased his 30-30 out of the scabbard just in case. He always trusted Slim and BC's senses because they were a lot more acute than his. Doug urged Slim up the trail, what there was of it, which was very rough and took considerable concentration to navigate while keeping his eyes peeled for possible danger. He had gone only another hundred yards when Slim stiffened up and snorted while looking slightly to the left toward the bottom of the canyon. There half sitting, half hung up in the branches of a huge ponderosa deadfall, was a human body. There must have been some other smells too, because Slim didn't want any part of that place. Doug figured it was bear scent since Slim hated and feared them. He dismounted and tied the horse to a pinon tree that was beside the high trail.

BC and Doug scrambled down the slope on foot, with carbine ready and alert to any sign that might tell him what happened. It was hard to determine how long the body had been there, but he figured at least two or three weeks. The skull was pretty badly damaged and was laid back sort of hanging over a limb, the scalp torn loose with strands of reddish brown hair attached. The clothing was torn to shreds, hanging in strips from outstretched arms. The legs were spread slightly with heels dug into the gravel, and the jeans were ripped nearly off. Beside the boots was a 30-30 rifle with the stock broken and bent at a right angle to the rest of the gun. Several wild animals and birds had evidently had their way and there was not much meat left on the skeleton.

All of a sudden Doug froze. A flood of emotion hit him—memories of human remains torn apart, the carnage, the blood, the ravages of war. It had been ten years since Doug was in Korea, but the memories that never die came rushing back. It took several minutes for him to collect himself and begin searching the body. Doug found a wallet in the left front pocket of the jeans which confirmed that this was Jim Lackey, a government hunter who lived in those parts and whose job it was to keep the coyotes and other varmints from bothering the rancher's livestock too much. This time it looked like Lackey had tackled a varmint that didn't take too kindly to being bothered.

Doug looked around and tried to piece together what had happened. BC smelled every little bit of scent in the area. There was still evidence of a lot of blood on the body and scattered around the scene. He was sure most of it was Jim's but also thought that some of it might belong to a grizzly that had attacked him, for he surmised that's what took place. Upon examining the rifle he found the chamber and magazine empty. Lackey must have fired at the bear several times without delivering a kill shot. He examined the area thoroughly but didn't find any "brass"—empty cartridges. After looking for tracks, he figured the bear had gone up the canyon after the scuffle. Doug left everything just the way he found it, thinking the sheriff would want to investigate the scene.

Retrieving his horse, he proceeded up the canyon and finally topped out after considerable difficulty. He had anticipated finding the dead bear's carcass somewhere up the canyon, but no scavenger birds like magpies or ravens could be seen. He couldn't imagine that a bear could travel that far with so much lead in him, assuming Lackey had hit his mark. Proceeding on the game trail for a bit after topping out, he saw claw marks on a patch of ground. Doug dismounted to examine this more closely, walking very slowly and leading his horse, looking for more sign. He noticed a small blood stain on a downed log which the bear had crawled over. There wasn't very much blood, which indicated that the bear wasn't hurt that badly.

Suddenly off to his right he caught a glimpse of movement and a cow elk appeared followed by a large herd. They were moving at a steady pace and were not panicked, passing from right to left about fifty yards in front of Doug. Approximately a hundred elk drifted by, with a bunch of spikes and young bulls bringing up the rear. There are a lot of elk and deer in this country as well as black bear, cougars, bobcats, and coyotes. Doug found no more animal sign, so he circled back, staying on top of the ridge as much as possible, heading for the line shack where he was temporarily living. He knew he should notify the sheriff of his discovery as soon as he could.

Doug was working as a cowhand on a ranch in Colorado that had a large section of high country which went all the way up to timberline and higher. This afforded some excellent summer pasture for a few thousand mama cows. These cows were trail drove to this summer range as soon as enough snow had melted to let the grass start to green. Most of the cows already had calves, while others would calve when they got to the summer pasture.

His line shack was nothing to brag about. It was a long, low wood frame building with a room at one end for a cowhand to sleep in. This room was equipped with a cot, a wood burning cookstove, a table, and some chairs made from rough sawmill lumber. A couple of packing crates were nailed to the wall for cabinets. The roof on the whole building was tin, and the sound could be deafening if you were inside during a heavy rain or hail storm. The other end of the building was a horse barn, with a small room for saddles, tack, and some grain in a barrel to keep the mice out.

A pipe carried water to the building, running from a spring that was up the side of the mountain behind the line shack. This pipe entered the back wall of the building and fed a faucet over a sink on the bunkhouse side, as well as running into a trough for keeping things cool and filling a water tub on the barn side. The excess water flowed downhill in front of the building to fill a small dirt tank. The person assigned to this line shack had a big responsibility, because he was tasked with the care of about two thousand mama cows and their calves.

The year was 1960, and Doug had survived the Korean War as a foot soldier. His left leg suffered a serious wound, but after a couple years of rehab with the VA he was back to almost normal except for a limp. He was six foot tall, about one-ninety with a lot of his weight in the shoulders and arms. He had light brown hair, blue eyes, slim waist, and as some ladies said, "a butt that would fit in a teacup," which was typical of many men who spent a lot of time in the saddle. He was good looking in a rugged sort of way, and physically strong—his only weakness being his left leg. Doug was born in northern Kansas on a ranch where his father and mother both worked. Like a lot of ranch hands, his parents moved around a lot and were now living near Jackson Hole, Wyoming. Doug had gone to school in several states, finally graduating from high school in Walsenburg, Colorado.

He had been working on the Circle Cross Ranch going on eight years now. The mama cows had to be checked almost daily to see if any needed help calving, making sure none were bogged down at a watering place, and watching for any of the many other maladies that a cow critter could get into. Most of the calving was accomplished in late January or early February, but since the bulls were left with the cows longer on this ranch to make sure all cows were bred, there were usually some late deliveries.

One dreaded problem was that there were still grizzly bears in the high country. Cow meat is a tasty treat to a grizzly, and they find cattle fairly easy to catch. A grizzly can outrun a good horse, so it can catch a cow with little effort. There were few grizzlies left in this country, but every now and then one would pass through and molest the cattle.

When Doug returned to the line shack that day he was one worried cowpoke. He definitely needed to get word to headquarters so they could notify the sheriff, and the ramrod—as the ranch foreman is called hereabouts—would have to decide if Doug needed help dealing with the grizzly. Ranch headquarters was about twenty miles away through pretty rough country, and it would take the better part of a day to get there horseback.

There was another line camp about ten miles away that had an old stone house occupied in the summer by a cowhand and his family. These folks also had a vehicle because there was a pig trail of a road to their camp, although the vehicle was an old unreliable Dodge pickup. They also had a telephone but the wires were strung through trees and on fence posts so it was inoperable much of the time. Doug decided if he left early he could make a sweep through part of the area he was responsible for and arrive at the Sweetwater camp by noon.

Sweetwater was manned by John Latham, his wife Sonja, their son Albert, age twelve, and two daughters, Lori, age ten, and Kelly, age eight. Doug decided that once he got there he could call HQ if the phone was working, or drive out for help. At first light he set off riding Big Red, a tall sorrel horse on his string, because Slim was tired from his long ordeal the day before. Doug had several horses on his string, including a pack mule named Festus who would pack all his supplies into this remote camp. Big Red had been a stud and acquired a lot of growth before being proud cut about age four, and in many ways he still acted like a stud. He was so muscled up that he jerked riders around a lot, and his trot was atrocious. But he could pull anything as long as the rope or cinch didn't break. BC came along for the trip, too.

Doug made a long arc, checking lots of cows on the way. They all seemed content and were licking each other, with the calves running and jumping and having a good time. Things looked very peaceful. As he approached Sweetwater camp, though, something didn't feel right. There was no sign of anyone and Ollie, the Latham's blue heeler, was not barking. Ollie was one of those dogs that knew when someone or something was approaching the place before anyone else did, and he would let you know about it. Doug figured John was out checking cows and had the dog with him.

As he got close to the yard, which was between the barn and the house, BC started growling and raising his hackles. Big Red started walking stiff-legged, arching his neck, with ears pointed and nostrils flared. Knowing how hard Big Red could pitch when he wanted to, Doug decided to get off and walk them in. Close to the barn he noticed a patch of blue, and as he approached he saw that it was Ollie. The dog was dead and several chunks of flesh were missing as if he had been partially eaten.

Doug was really worried now, and he ran to the house, calling out and pounding on the door. He noticed that there were some deep scratches on the heavy hardwood, which could only have been made by powerful blows. The door flung open and there was Latham's son Albert with an old pistol in his hand and a wild look in his eyes.

He cried out, "Daddy's been nearly kilt by a bear."

When Doug stepped in, Sonja was sitting in a rocker by the fireplace with a terrified look on her face and the two girls came running up to him, all talking at the same time.

"Daddy's been hurt bad—do something, Doug."

He went to the bedroom and saw John lying on the bed,

his left pant leg ripped and the leg badly mangled. He had deep claw marks on his face and chest. Some of his wounds had been washed and bandaged.

"John?"

John opened his eyes and looked up. "Doug."

"I didn't think they could hurt you with an ax."

John tried to grin but gave it up because it hurt too badly.

"Looks like you came up against a purty tough hombre this time, John?"

"Yeah."

"Well, you're better off than Jim Lackey," Doug said.

He looked at Doug with a question in his eyes.

"I found Lackey yesterday way up in that broke off country below Sangre de Cristo Peak. Looks like he'd been killed by a grizzly."

"Damn," John spat, with a cough.

Doug went on, "He got off a few shots, but I never did find the dead bear."

"When?" John asked.

"I figure about two to three weeks ago."

The kids had all crowded into the bedroom and looking at Albert, Doug asked,

"Is the phone working?"

"Yep," he said. "We called Dub about two hours ago."

"They should be getting here any time now," Doug replied. "What happened here?"

"Last night about three in the morning Ollie started barking like crazy, the horses that were in the corral were raising hell, the milk cow was bawling, so daddy pulled on his pants and boots, grabbed his shotgun, and went outside," Albert explained excitedly.

John took a deep breath and said hoarsely, "I went out but couldn't see anything. Ollie was by the barn door barking and snarling at something. As I got closer Ollie started backing up. About then this huge creature came rushing at us and swatted Ollie like he was a fly, then kept coming toward me. I raised my shotgun and fired but the thing knocked me flat on my back and proceeded to maul me purty good. Albert came out of the house and fired that ol' pistol a time or two, and the critter ran off. I ain't never seen anything that big and ugly, Doug!"

"Did you hit him, Albert?" Doug asked.

"I don't think so. I just wanted him to get off daddy," he replied.

"So you all got your daddy in the house. Then what happened?"

"The bear came back and tried to get in the door. We had it bolted and the bear finally left. Momma's been so scared she just sits in that rocker and moans," Albert said.

"You kids done well. I'm so proud of you," Doug said.

John's face displayed another one of those weak grins. Directly they heard BC barking in the yard, so Doug went out to investigate. It was Dub, the ranch foreman, coming up the road in his four-wheel-drive pickup. Behind him was a sheriff's vehicle with a deputy driving. When they pulled into the yard everything was explained to them and Dub suggested the first thing they should do was get John to a hospital. He said the ambulance was about five miles down the road and couldn't make it any further. The mattress with John on it was carefully loaded in the back of the sheriff's vehicle, with the rest of the family divided between the two vehicles.

The deputy was Harlan Martinez, whom Doug had known for many years. Doug punched cows with Harlan's father, Martine, several years ago. Harlan and Doug worked on ranches together in the summer while they were in high school, but afterward—being wiser than the rest of the cowboys—Harlan went off to university and got a good education in law enforcement. He was now the deputy sheriff for this area, being stationed in La Veta.

Doug told him about finding Jim Lackey, and Harlan said that explained why Lackey had been missing for several weeks. He said he figured something like this may have happened. Someone had found Jim's pickup and horse trailer at the mouth of Echo Canyon, which was ten to twelve miles from where Doug found the body. His horse had come into another camp called Sunnyside, and was jaded with the saddle hanging off to one side.

Harlan and Doug quickly studied a topographical map and discussed the best way to get vehicles as close as possible to the site. Doug volunteered to meet them at the chosen spot the next day and lead them to the body. He then put out plenty of hay for John's horses and they had water in the corral. The calf was put in the barn with its mother, the milk cow. Things should be okay for a few days unless the grizz came back.

As the vehicles rattled down the rough road Doug saddled Big Red, having turned him out in the corral, and with BC leading the way they headed for home. There was lots to think about on that ride. He now had two sections to keep an eye on until Dub could get a replacement for John, and now there was a wounded grizzly in the area. It was late when Doug arrived at his camp, and after feeding the horses and doing chores he fell into bed exhausted.

The next morning Doug started off again at first light, wishing that someday maybe he could get more sleep and set off at second light. He was riding a beautiful bay horse named Frog Honey who had an easy ground-covering gait that quickly put on lots of miles. He was the best horse on his string for working cows. Doug kept his eyes peeled for bear sign along the way and checked any cattle he came across. Everything was peaceful, just the way a cowboy likes to see things.

He arrived at the meeting place and waited a couple of hours before he heard the sheriff's vehicle laboring up the canyon. There were five men and they were all afoot since they didn't bring a horse trailer with them. It took them about two hours to get to the body and some of the out-of-shape city boys were having a tough time of it. They searched the area and investigated the corpse, put several items in forensics bags, took a lot of pictures, finally placing the remains into a body bag. Using a litter, they carried everything back to their vehicle. Doug didn't even ask how they were going to get all that stuff and themselves back to their office, for he figured they were big boys and could work it out somehow. He said his good-byes and headed out to make his rounds.

The next morning, back on ol' Slim, he began a wide sweep, staying higher up than two days ago and hoping to arrive at Sweetwater later in the day. He crossed several long grassy draws, checking the cows in each one and making sure none were bogged down in the mud at a water hole. As he entered one of these grassy draws about mid-morning, he was surprised that he didn't see any cows. He thought this was unusual and started riding up the draw looking for cattle tracks. BC and Slim were getting nervous because they could smell something, and BC started scenting a trail through the grass and steadily moving up the draw.

As he was following BC, a movement caught Doug's eye. There in the timber at the head of the draw a magpie darted up with a hoarse cry. As Doug got closer he crossed a patch of torn up ground with tufts of grass scattered about. There was a lot of blood on the ground and smears of it on the grass, with a blood trail leading toward the timber. A little further up there were many more magpies and a few ravens. Suddenly a huge bald eagle flew up and was valiantly trying to take off, but he was so full he was having a hard time of it.

This was about all Slim wanted of this place. As he was getting very spooky, Doug tied him securely to a tree and proceeded on foot with carbine in hand. In the tall grass he found a cow that had been killed and mostly eaten. There was a lot of sign around the kill indicating that a huge bear had been there. To make sure it was a bear that killed the cow, Doug checked the head and saw the tell-tale bite marks on the nose, and he lifted the head to determine if the neck was broken. He knew that most of the time when a bear makes a kill it will stay nearby until it's all consumed. He kept a sharp lookout and backed out of there very carefully.

BC wanted to trail on up the mountain, but Doug called

him back and made him stay close. He mounted up and continued checking other meadows and more cattle, arriving at Sweetwater late in the afternoon. He decided to spend the night there, get the chores done, and let the horses and milk cow out of the corral to fend for themselves. They wouldn't go far since there was always the potential of a bit of grain if they stayed close to camp.

In the house Doug tried the telephone and found it to be working. After several rings Dub answered and they caught each other up on recent developments. John was in hospital and was to have several surgeries. He was weak but doing as well as could be expected. Sonja and the kids, when not at hospital, stayed at their winter home in town. Sonja had pulled herself together and was functioning again, but swore she would never go back to the mountains. Dub suggested that they hire a hunter with bear hounds to track down the grizz, and Doug added that he should have some good fighting dogs as well as hounds because this bear was wounded and terribly fierce.

Next morning the phone rang while Doug was eating his breakfast. It was Dub saying he just made arrangements for a hunter with bear dogs who would arrive at Sweetwater later that day or early the next morning. Doug said he would be out checking cows today, but he'd be back to Sweetwater before dark.

That day Doug rode out to check the southern end of John's range and he found only one problem—a cow had given birth to a calf, but a pair of coyotes had fought and distracted the cow until they were able to kill the calf. She had a tight bag and had not cleaned the placenta properly, so Doug had to rope her and tie her down so he could tend to her. BC had run the coyotes off so Doug didn't even get a proper shot at them. When he left the mama cow she was standing over the carcass of her calf, bawling. Doug was hoping he could get that cow together with the calf of the cow that had been killed by the bear, but he would have to deal with that later.

When he was nearly back to Sweetwater he could hear a vehicle growling and pulling up the steep road to the camp. Soon a big four-wheel-drive pickup pulling a horse trailer jolted into the yard. In the back of the truck was a dog box with a bunch of dogs. BC was going crazy—he had not had this much company in a long time. The owner of this outfit was Bobby Daugherty, a hunter whom Doug had once met. After getting the horses and dogs settled, and rustling up some grub for themselves, they sat on a bench in front of the house and Doug told Bobby all that had happened.

Drawing a map in the dust on the ground he pointed out where everything had taken place. Bobby remarked that if the grizz headed up into that rough country above timberline they would probably lose him because there were so many rock slides with big cracks and caves for underground hiding places. They decided to start in the morning near the cow carcass in hopes that the bear had come back to feed.

The next morning they set off, again at first light, and rode in silence for about an hour. It was cooler than normal at this altitude and Doug's Levi jacket felt purty good. As they approached the bear kill Bobby's dogs, especially his lead dog Sally, were getting excited. They nosed around the kill a while and soon Sally gave out her beautiful bawl that sounded like a bugle being blown. The music of trail hounds giving voice when on the scent is enough to give you cold shivers and make your hair stand up.

Sally was about one hundred yards up the side of the mountain in the timber. Bobby had four trail hounds and four Airedales, two of those being crossbred with hounds. An Airedale is a fierce fighter when facing critters like bear or cougar. They don't have the scent ability of a hound, but once the trail warms and they can smell the quarry, they will run with their heads up, scenting the air, and outrunning the hounds. Airedales have some ferocious teeth in powerful jaws that can inflict quite a bit of damage when they bite. They save a lot of hounds from injury when the critter being chased decides to fight it out on the ground.

Most critters are smart enough to go up a tree if they can't outrun the dogs. A grizz usually won't climb a tree once it's full grown, but can climb a rocky bluff like a cat. Soon Sally had help from the other hounds. They found that the trail was cold, so the bear had not come back to this kill. The hounds kept trailing up and slightly below the high ridge on their right. Farther down to the left was a deep canyon, so the riders decided to stay on the ridge in order to hear better. The dogs kept going generally in the same direction for about a mile when suddenly their voices changed and the riders could tell they were a lot more excited.

"They found where he was laid up," Bobby said.

Their direction changed, too, as they began trailing toward the riders but a little higher up. The men and horses kept climbing the ridge and were getting closer to the sound of the pack.

"There they are, up ahead," Bobby said excitedly.

Now Doug could see the dogs moving through the trees, running from left to right. When they got to where the dogs had crossed their trail, they looked for tracks and finally found a rear foot imprint of a large grizzly in the soft dirt. The hounds continued trailing around a huge shoulder of the mountain, going away from them and gradually getting a little higher.

When the riders got to the apex of the ridge they could hear the dogs up to their right, and suddenly the whole pack was screaming at the top of their lungs. The Airedales were yapping, which they don't do until they have the bear in sight. Everything was moving at a very fast pace now. The men were riding as fast as they could, trying to stay within earshot of the dogs. BC, who had elected to stay with Doug, was having a hard time keeping up. They soon came up against some high rocky bluffs that ran along the side of the mountain. It slowed their progress as there were a lot of boulders, rocks, and scree at the base of these bluffs. The horses had to pick their way through this mess, and fortunately both of these horses were good rock-rollers. That is what a horse is called when he can get through rough country like a mule.

They continued ahead as best they could, finally coming to a place where the bluff turned a corner. After they got around this corner they could hear the dogs further up the mountain in a shallow draw, and it sounded like a terrible fight was going on. Because this place formed a natural amphitheater, the sound echoed down to the men so they could hear everything that was going on. One of the dogs let out a blood-curdling scream and Bobby said,

"It's killing my dogs—we got to get up there!"

The going was rougher with every step, so they decided to tie the horses, take their guns and ropes and whatever they thought they would need, and go forward on foot. It wasn't much easier on foot but they hurried as fast as they could. When they approached the site of the melee, a breeze blew up the canyon and must have carried the men's scent to the bear because he decided to quit the fight and run for it. The only way out was up the cliff behind him—which is where he went, leaving the dogs far below.

When Doug and Bobby arrived on the scene the bear was gone. There were some injured dogs to care for and get back to camp. Several of the dogs had cuts, some were limping, and one had a fractured spine. Bobby put this dog out of its misery and they struggled back to the horses, leading as many dogs as they could.

"Where that grizz is headed is some mighty rough country. I would have lost more dogs had we stayed after him," Bobby muttered.

On the way back to Sweetwater they crossed one of those grassy swales and out in the middle of it was a cinnamon colored bear of the Black Bear species. He was a two-year-old and not full grown yet. The dogs had seen him about the same time as the men and the race was on. He ran about a half mile before going up a huge Ponderosa pine tree, sitting on a big limb about twenty feet from the ground. He was whining and popping his teeth, showing his displeasure at being disturbed. Bobby called the dogs off the tree and continued toward camp leaving the young bear to contemplate his situation alone.

When they arrived at Sweetwater it was late and they tended to the doctoring, feeding, and getting dogs and horses settled in for the night. As Doug fixed supper they discussed the hunt.

"I hope that bear just keeps going over the divide and finds a more friendly place on the other side of these mountains," Doug said.

"That would be nice, but he knows there is plenty of food available on this side, so I'd bet he'll be back," Bobby replied.

"The cattle business is tough enough, but a bear like that can kill off the net profit in short order."

"Anybody fool enough to go into the cow business is a gambler at heart. He might as well go to Vegas and put it all on a roll of the dice."

"Yeah, but it's a good life. I love it up here in the mountains. When I see young calves running, jumping, and playing on a sunny morning I get a swelling in my chest."

"Probably indigestion from eating your own cooking," Bobby said, laughing. "How come you never took up with a woman?"

"I did once. After I got back from Korea I had a bum leg from shrapnel and was going through rehab at the VA in Colorado Springs. I met this cute as a button little blond rehab nurse. We got along purty good and had a lot of laughs. When I got out of the hospital I got a job as a truck driver. I moved in with her, since she had a little apartment there in Colorado Springs. We were doing purty good when I discovered that she had a lot of other admirers. If they would come around and I was there she would tell them that she had me and they weren't welcome, which made me feel real proud. But one day I came home from work and caught her in bed with one of her supposed exes. He was a hippie and a druggie so it hurt purty bad. I did what most men do—got drunk. Next day I got my gear and came up here. I asked Dub for a job and I've been here ever since."

"Wow! I can understand how that must have soured you on women, but they are not all like that."

"Yeah, there are lots of good women in the world. I just haven't met the right one yet."

"Hopefully you will someday."

"I don't know. I have a good dog and a string of good ponies who are all loyal to me and don't ask for much. Ol' BC there is about the most loyal friend a man could have."

BC, who was curled up on the rug in front of the fireplace, raised his head and looked at Doug quizzically.

"Why do you call that dog BC?" Bobby asked.

"He's a Border Collie, ain't he?"

"Oh, I get it."

How about you, Bobby? Did you ever marry?" Doug wondered.

"Yes, Jennifer and I have been married about ten years and have two kids. We have a little eighty-acre place down near Red Wing and have a good hunting business going. I take on about twenty elk hunters a year, about a dozen deer hunters, and several bear and mountain lion hunters. We won't get rich but it pays the bills. It wouldn't be possible without Jennifer—she's the catalyst. She keeps everything organized, cooks for the hunters, tends the kids, gardens, takes care of the stock, and can ride and shoot as good as anyone. I do my bit when I'm home, but when I am out with hunters she holds down the fort."

"Wow," Doug said. "You are a lucky man."

Staring up at the ceiling Bobby asked, "By the way, what's the story on this house? It's a long way from nowhere."

"Well, the way I understand it, a feller came up here about fifty years ago to set up a ranch. His wife refused to live in a shack so he built this fine stone house for her. It was way too far from town so she lasted about a year. He stayed on for another twenty years or so before starving out. The Circle Cross bought it about then. It's been used as a line camp for years. They usually put a family in here for the summer and some of them have really enjoyed it. I don't think John's wife liked it much, though."

"Why do they call it Sweetwater?

"That water out yonder in the spring is as nice as any water in this country." After a short pause, Doug asked, "Is Dub going to pay you for your services? I know you lost a valuable dog today?"

"Only if we kill the bear. That's the deal."

"So are you coming back?"

"I've got to go home and let these dogs heal up. Then I'll be back if the bear comes back—you'll have to let me know."

"Don't worry, if he shows up again someone will call you."

After the supper dishes were done, Bobby rolled out his bed on the floor. Doug went to bed in Albert's room. Next morning after breakfast, Bobby loaded up all his belongings and headed down the rugged road. Doug saddled up ol' Slim and, although the horse was still tired, they made a sweep through some lower foothills that he hadn't checked in a while. They had a leisurely day and got back to their camp in early afternoon.

Sheriff's Deputy Harlan Martinez found out that Jim Lackey lived in Walsenburg, so he went there the day after they brought the body out of the mountains. The corpse was still at the coroner's office/clinic in La Veta. When he found the Lackey house it looked like a little run-down, nondescript house in a poorer part of town. He knocked on the door several times and was beginning to think no one was home when the door suddenly flew open. There stood a woman of medium height with mousy brown hair, slender, with unusually large breasts. She had an angry look on her face, as if she had been disturbed and didn't appreciate it. She glanced at his badge and uniform disapprovingly.

"What do you want?"

"Mrs. Lackey?" Harlan asked.

"Who wants to know?" she blurted belligerently.

"I'm Harlan Martinez from the sheriff's department and I need to talk to Mrs. Lackey." Harlan showed her his badge.

"It's about Jim ain't it? I knew when he didn't come home something was up."

"May I come in, ma'am, and I'll explain everything?"

"No, you can't. I just don't allow strangers in my house!"

Harlan happened to glance over the woman's left shoulder and saw a boot, but only for a few seconds before the boot was pulled back out of his view. It was a cowboy boot—a high-top with jeans stuffed inside—an expensive boot with red dye and fancy stitching.

"Ma'am, I'm just doing my job. I have some bad news. Are you Jim's wife?"

"Yes?"

"Ma'am, I'm sorry to have to inform you that your husband is dead."

Harlan was studying her face and the only hint of emotion he could see was a slight twitch at the corner of her mouth.

"What happened?"

"Your husband was evidently killed a few weeks ago in the mountains by a bear, right about the time you reported him missing."

"He was often gone for weeks at a time—not always hunting and trapping. I'm purty sure he had a girlfriend down in Trinidad."

"Ma'am we need you to come by the coroner's office to identify the body. Also, we need your permission to do an autopsy to determine for sure what killed your husband. Is that okay?"

"Do whatever the hell you want to do," she said shoving the door shut.

"Well, that was certainly an unusual turn of events," Harlan mused while getting in his vehicle and turning into the road. Evidently she is getting a bit on the side, too.

The next morning Harlan got a call from the coroner who asked him to stop by his office. After finishing some of his duties, he arrived there a little before noon. The coroner said he had something interesting to show him, and he led the way to the autopsy room.

"When I was digging around in there," waving a hand toward the torso, "I found a fragment of lead. I kept digging and found more fragments and a chunk embedded in the spine. If a bear killed Mr. Lackey, then he must have been carrying a black powder rifle or pistol, 44 caliber or bigger I'd guess. Also, I think the skull injuries might be from the stock of that rifle." He pointed to the broken rifle lying on a table. "What I'd like to do is send the body and all the evidence bags to the state crime lab at Denver. It's obvious that a bear and other animals were feeding on the body, but I don't think that's what killed him. The lab can help sort that out."

"Wow! A murder," exclaimed Harlan, as they walked back to the doctor's office. "I never even suspected. I'll contact the DA for permission and have his office call you."

Bidding the coroner goodbye, Harlan drove to the Justice Center and explained the details of the case to the sheriff. Then they both went to the DA's office and did likewise there. Afterward Harlan made several phone calls, including one to Dub Ethridge, the ramrod at the Circle Cross.

A few days later Harlan went to the Busy Bee Café in La Veta to have some coffee and breakfast. As he entered, he glanced around to see who else was there. Out of the corner of his eye he noticed a boot. "Now, I know that boot," he mused to himself. There under a table in one of the booths, was the boot he had seen at Lackey's house. The boot was on a foot and leg attached to the local cattle brand inspector, Jim Rice. Rice was a big man, quite handsome, and according to local gossip, quite a lady's man. He had worked as a cowhand for many years in Colorado and New Mexico. A few years ago he applied for a job as a brand inspector and got it. He was the only black brand inspector in the state.

Changing his mind about where to sit, Harlan eased over to Jim's table and said, "Good morning, Jim. Mind if I join you?"

"Suit yourself," Jim said. "I'd enjoy the company."

After the usual chit-chat about the weather and cattle prices, Harlan asked, "Did you hear about Jim Lackey?"

"Yeah, gossip has it a bear done him in. What a horrible way to go."

"Sure is. Me and some of the boys had to go up in that canyon and bring him out. It was plenty horrible."

"Who found him? That's some purty wild country up there?"

"Doug Jepsen—he rides for the Circle Cross and works out of Granger cow camp."

"Yeah, I know Doug. Good hand. I ain't ever been to that camp, though. I know it's a long way back in there. There's not a road to that camp is there?"

"No, the only way in is horseback. They have to pack everything in. The way I understand it there was a road when the camp was built, but that was back in the forties when that country was logged. The old roadbed is all washed out or grown over now."

"That's got to get mighty lonely up there all by yourself all summer."

"I'm sure it is, but Doug seems to enjoy it. Where you been working lately, Jim?"

"Oh, all over. I've got a big area to cover. I've been over by Rocky Ford, Trinidad, and a few weeks ago I was over by Alamosa for a week or so."

Harlan was wondering if this last bit of information was given intentionally as an implied alibi.

"Well, I've got to go check some cows up by Cuchara this morning," Jim said, throwing some money on the table. "You take care, Harlan," and out the door he went.

Harlan puzzled over this for a moment but was interrupted by other coffee drinkers and gossipers who wanted to visit and pump him for information about Lackey.

In the meantime Doug was keeping a close watch on the cattle for fear that the grizz might come back. He checked the grassy valleys that ran up close to timberline almost every day. One day he headed over toward Sweetwater and as he approached he discovered someone was living there. He could see a different pickup in the yard, different horses in the corral, and a different dog. When Doug rode in he recognized it was Fro Walden's dog, horses, and pickup.

The dog came running toward them, and he and BC got reacquainted with a lot of hackles raised, growling, and sniffing. They soon figured out they knew each other and were happy to meet again. Fro and his wife were unloading stuff from the pickup and carrying things into the house. After greeting each other, Doug caught them up on what he knew and they caught him up on what they knew.

Before they left headquarters Dub had informed them about the latest news that Harlan had given him. Doug was shocked when he heard about the bullet being found in Lackey's body. He racked his brain to try and remember anything he had seen that would suggest that someone else had been up in that canyon. He couldn't remember anything. Of course, considerable time had passed after the killing until he found the body.

"So you all going to be up here for the rest of the summer?" he asked.

"Yep. John is going to be a long time healing, and I'm not sure if he'll ever be able to ride again," Fro replied.

"Oh man, that would be terrible. John was born in the saddle."

"Yeah, I just hope and pray he'll be okay."

"What about your camp? Who's going to take care of it?"

"Dub has some teenagers down there now, and he thinks he can handle it with their help."

"Why doesn't he hire another hand?"

"Can't afford it, he claims. He's already worried about the bottom line. Says he can't take on any more expense."

"Come and get it," Fro's wife Julie called from the door. "It's not much, but you're welcome to join us. I made a batch of green chili stew before we came up here and I just heated it up."

Fro and Julie had been living at Sunnyside camp, which was lower down in the foothills. He had calved out a bunch of heifers earlier in the year and was taking care of them there on a spread of about five or six square miles, which was not quite as large an area as was worked by the rest of the hands.

"Do you remember when John shot that odd critter last spring?" Fro asked with a chuckle while they ate lunch.

"Ha, yeah, that was something, wasn't it?" Doug replied.

Fro was referring to one day during the spring gather when everyone had gone to the cookhouse at headquarters for the noon meal. Since the meal was not ready yet, John, Fro, and Doug went to a big Quonset barn where a lot of ranch machinery and equipment was stored. They needed the sprayer, which was on a two-wheeled trailer with a large tank for the solution the cowhands sprayed on the cattle. All the stock were run through a dip tank or sprayed before going to summer pasture to keep the flies and parasites off. This sprayer was used when there was a gathering of cattle at a place that didn't have a dip tank. It had a pump powered by a small gasoline engine.

As they walked into the barn, a small critter came running out from behind a hay machine and scampered across the floor. Quick as a flash John whipped out his pistol from his chap pocket and shot the critter through the head. After getting the sprayer untangled and out of the barn they went back to the cookhouse, John carrying his trophy kill. He dropped it on the ground where all the rest of the hands were sitting.

"Doug, you know a lot about critters—what the hell is that?" he asked.

"John, best I can figure is you've killed a critter that is on the endangered species list," Doug answered. "It's a Black-Footed Ferret."

"Really! I hope no one here reports me."

"As long as you have that pistol in your leggins pocket, I don't think we'll be saying a word," Doug joked.

After the dinner as everyone was filing out of the cookhouse a car pulled up. It was a very pretty neighbor lady that lived about a mile down the road in one of the rented houses owned by the ranch.

"You all haven't seen my pet ferret have you?" she asked. "He got out of the house and I can't find him anywhere."

You have never seen a more dumb-looking bunch of cowboys in your life. All staring at each other and shuffling their feet and saying, "No ma'am, we haven't seen anything." One of the younger cowboys even offered to go help her look for it, but Dub intervened and said his services were needed elsewhere. After she left, everyone was sworn to secrecy.

"I have to laugh every time I think about that," Fro said.

"You mean you never did tell that poor girl what happened to her pet?" Julie asked.

"Hell no—you think we're crazy? As far as I know she still don't know," Doug added.

As they were going outside and Doug was putting on his hat, Fro remarked, "What's that on your hat? Looks like cow shit."

"It is cow shit," he said. "I decided to ride Pingo this morning 'cuz he hasn't been rode in about a week, and as we were leaving camp I touched him with my spur and he broke in two. He pitched so hard that he threw me plumb over his head and I landed right on top of my hat in a fresh cowpie. I think I jarred something loose in my neck."

Fro had a good laugh. "I thought you were a better bronc buster than that."

"I am, but he took me by surprise," Doug exclaimed sheepishly. "By the way, Fro, when Lackey's horse came into your camp what did it look like? Were there any blood stains or anything unusual?" Doug asked, trying to change the subject. "I've been puzzling over this."

"The horse didn't come into camp. Actually, I found it up the draw at the windmill that's about a half mile from the camp—the one that has a steel tub by the pump. He was standing under that ponderosa there by the windmill."

"Was the horse dragging its reins?"

"No, the saddle was a little off to the side because the cinch was loose. The bridle was hanging from the saddle horn and was actually tied on by the saddle rope's latch string. There were no blood stains on the saddle or anything else out of the ordinary. In fact the horse is still at Sunnyside, since no one came to claim it."

"I find that really odd. I doubt if Lackey loosened the cinch and took off the bridle, and turned the horse loose before he was killed." Doug said, "I need to talk to Harlan, but I probably won't get the chance until we get all the cattle out of the mountains. Do you want me to show you where that bear killed the cow?" Doug asked.

"Draw me a map. I can figure it out," Fro replied.

So back at the bench in front of the house Doug drew a map in the dust on the ground, pointing out where everything had happened over the last week or so. They agreed that if they needed to get word to each other, they would leave a note in a tobacco can that was nailed to a post halfway between the two cow camps. This post had a tub wired to it, made out of an old tire turned inside out. The tub contained salt and mineral for the cattle and was replenished about once a month, carried in by pack horse or mule.

Harlan was at his desk doing paperwork about a month later, when he picked up the case file on the Lackey murder and began reading through it again. Something caught his eye this time through. Lackey's wife made a statement that Lackey had a girlfriend in Trinidad. He wondered if there was something to that. He decided to call the sheriff, Edwardo Sisneros, and discuss it with him. Harlan had a lot of respect for the sheriff and his investigative abilities. "Ed is plenty shrewd," he thought. "I'll run it by him." He was lucky to catch the sheriff in his office when he phoned.

> "I'm glad you called," Ed said. "I just saw the report from the crime lab, and they're purty sure the death was caused by a gunshot wound from a high caliber black powder weapon. The bullet was beat up purty bad, but they think it could be from a fifty caliber. Have you checked out everyone on the Circle Cross to see if anyone had a motive?"

"Yes, I have, and nothing. I've known most of these people all my life and can vouch for them. I'm confident none of them were involved with Lackey's murder. Their only contact with him was occasionally in his profession as a government hunter. Two things intrigue me, though. First, at Lackey's house I saw a boot, which I later saw Jim Rice wearing. And second, Mrs. Lackey's statement that her husband was seeing someone in Trinidad."

"Hmm, yes, that's very interesting. Can you place Jim Rice anywhere near the murder scene?"

"No, he made a vague statement that he was working near Alamosa at that time."

"How about the wife? Could she have killed him?" Ed asked.

"I don't think so. According to the neighbors she never goes anywhere except to work and shopping once in a while. She has a job at a bar in Walsenburg and is there most of the time even when she is not on duty. She was in town when the killing supposedly took place," Harlan explained.

"She could have got someone else to do it for her."

"I suppose. I'm still following up several leads."

"Do you think this Trinidad angle should be checked out?"

"It has been giving me an itch. I think we should investigate it."

"Then you better scratch it. No stone unturned and all that."

"I'll go there tomorrow," Harlan said, and then hung up.

On his way to the Las Animas County Sheriff's office in Trinidad the next day, Harlan called the dispatcher who transferred his call to one of the deputies. Harlan knew deputy Frank Lucero from his university days.

"Hey, Frank, how's it going?" Harlan asked.

"Harlan, good to hear from you. How's the wife?"

"The wife's fine, I'm fine. I'm on my way to Trinidad as we speak."

"You coming to visit me? Well, I'm impressed."

"Yeah, that plus I'm working on a case and I wanted to see if it was all right if I go poking around in your jurisdiction?"

"What are you working on? How can I help?"

"It's a murder case—a guy was found dead in the mountains and there is a possibility that he had been in Trinidad before his death. I just need to check it out."

"Sure, it's fine, and if I can help just let me know. Today I've got a full plate and won't be able to go with you, but if you run into a snag, call me on the radio—I'm unit nine."

"Thanks Frank, I'll let you know what I find out," Harlan said, signing off.

Arriving in Trindad about mid-morning, and knowing that Lackey liked to have a beer once in a while, Harlan started in some of the bars and saloons to show Lackey's picture to bartenders and waitresses. After visiting several bars and restaurants he found a couple of people who recognized Lackey but couldn't remember ever seeing him with anyone. In the afternoon Harlan went to a cantina in the Latino section of town. He entered, waiting for his eyes to adjust to the dark interior, and smelled the rank odors of booze and cigarettes. He approached the bar near the waitress call station and waited for the bartender who was visiting with a couple of regulars down the bar.

"Can I help you?" A woman stepped up beside him.

She looked to be in her late forties or early fifties and her face showed the lines of many hard years. Evidently she had once been pretty, but the prolonged effects of a hard life were catching up to her. She was looking at Harlan's uniform with a question in her eyes.

"Do you work here?" he asked.

"Yeah, name's Rosa. That's my husband Mike," nodding her head toward the bartender. "We own this place."

"I'm Harlan Martinez from Huerfano County. I'm trying to find information about this man," he answered, first showing his shield and then the picture of Lackey.

He had obtained the picture from Lackey's personnel file at the US Fish and Wildlife Service.

"Huerfano County. You're a little off your beat, ain't you?"

"Yeah, well, we have to go wherever we have a lead."

"Yes, I know this man. His name is Jim and he always sits at that table. He'll come in several days in a row, then disappear for about a month or so, then he'll be back."

"Does he ever have anyone with him or does he meet anyone here?"

"Yeah," she chuckled, "he meets someone all right. He is sweet on Anita, one of our waitresses. He's always showing her a lot of attention and sometimes he waits until she gets off work and they leave together."

"How long has this romance been going on?"

"About a year, although I haven't seen him in must be over a month now. He'll probably be showing up any day now."

"Is Anita here now?"

"No she doesn't come in until about seven when we get

busy."

"I really need to speak to her. Do you know where I can find her?"

"Yeah, she still lives at home with her family, but I would beware of those brothers of hers if I were you. They are a mean bunch. Her name is Anita Trujillo and this is her address." Rosa wrote the address on the back of a waitress ticket.

Harlan found the address with some difficulty and when pulling into the yard saw several vehicles—some derelict that had not been running in a long time, a couple of newer pickups, and three Harleys. He called the dispatcher at the local sheriff's office and told her where he was, and he requested that Frank call him on his radio in five minutes. He then switched the radio to loud speaker. As he was getting out of his unit he noticed three men, all probably in their twenties, sitting on the front porch, all with a can of beer in their hands. They were dressed in jeans and sleeveless undershirts or T-shirts with Harley logos. All of the exposed skin on their arms and necks was covered in tattoos. He stepped to the front of his unit.

"Is this the house where Anita Trujillo lives?" Harlan asked showing his shield.

"Who wants to know?" one of the young men who looked to be the oldest asked belligerently.

"I'm Harlan Martinez from the Huerfano County Sheriff's office and I'm investigating a case. It's possible Anita may have spoken to someone of interest when she was working at the cantina."

"She doesn't know nothing, and she doesn't want to talk to you."

"How could you possibly know that?" Harlan asked.

The man suddenly stood up and his two brothers did likewise. Harlan noticed all three of them were carrying pistols, two in holsters on their belts and one, the oldest man, had a .45 tucked behind his belt buckle.

"I only have a couple of questions for Anita. I can ask them here in your presence if that would be okay," Harlan stated.

"We don't talk to cops!" the oldest said, getting louder and angrier.

"Unit nine to Harlan Martinez," the loudspeaker on Harlan's unit blared.

"Excuse me," Harlan said, smiling at the three men on the porch, "I have to get this."

He got back in his unit and turned off the speaker, grabbed the mike and said, "This is Harlan—thanks for calling," as he backed his unit out of the yard and pulled away from the house.

"Where are you?" Frank asked.

"I've been talking to the Trujillo boys," Harlan replied.

"Harlan, you should never go there unless you have plenty of backup. Those people are mean as hell."

"So I noticed, I'm leaving there now."

"Are they involved in this murder you're investigating?"

"I don't know at this time. It may come to that before this is over."

"Don't go there again alone," Frank warned. "If you must go there, let me know and we'll take plenty of backup—the National Guard if need be."

"Thanks for the advice, partner. I'm going to stop by that cantina again and then head home. I'll call you later."

Harlan signed off. When he arrived at the cantina, several more customers were in the place. Rosa was busy waiting on a table so Harlan assumed his usual place at the bar beside the waitress station. Soon Mike, the owner, sauntered over. He was a big man who looked like he might have been a weightlifter at one time, but now his bulk was running more to the paunch.

"What can I get you?" he asked.

"I am Harlan Martinez, a sheriff's deputy, and I'd like to ask you some questions," Harlan said, showing his shield.

"Didn't you get enough answers when you were in here before?" Mike said, scowling toward Rosa.

"Just a couple more things. Did Jim Lackey ever meet anyone else when he was in here? Talk to anyone in particular?"

"He tried to put the move on a tall brunette one time when Anita wasn't here. But the woman wanted no part of him. He kept after her, and her boyfriend finally showed up and put a stop to it. I could hardly blame Jim. That woman was sure a looker."

"Had you seen that woman or her boyfriend in here before?"

"No, but one of the cowboys in here that night must have known him 'cuz he called him Sully. Sorry, but I've got customers waiting."

"Thanks for all your help," Harlan said as he turned and left the cantina.

Doug was riding his range one day and thinking. One thing about riding is that it gives a man a lot of time to think. He kept puzzling over the fact that there must have been another human being in the canyon where Lackey was killed that day. He knew he didn't remember seeing any tracks of men, and he wondered how someone could have gotten in there and out again without being seen.

If there were horses, it seemed reasonable that he would have seen horse tracks. Since Doug was in that area, he decided to ride over there and take another look. The dirt tank where he had seen the grizzly tracks was in a long grassy swale that sloped up toward the mouth of the canyon where he found the body. He started at the tank and crisscrossed the grassy meadow several times looking for horse tracks. The only ones he found were those of his own horse when he was there the day he found the body and the day the deputies removed the body.

When he got to the mouth of the canyon he turned left and rode along the edge of the meadow where the ground started rising steeply up the mountain toward treeline. Watching closely for any sign of tracks, he gave up after about four hundred yards and turned around to examine the right side of the canyon mouth. After riding along that side for about one hundred yards he saw the tracks of what looked like a large animal that came down the mountain and walked under a big Ponderosa tree and out onto the grass. He wasn't sure whether the tracks were made by an elk, a cow, or possibly a horse.

Dismounting, he tied his horse and examined the tracks. Under the tree the animal had sunk down into the mast—the pine needles and debris that accumulates in a forest—so it was impossible to determine what kind of animal made the track. Following the line the tracks were going, right at the edge of the grass in a bare spot he found the track of a shod horse. It was smaller than normal and could possibly be a pony track. There was only one track and it had been weathered by the thunderstorms which occurred several times since the assumed time of the death. The single track was partially protected by a tree.

Doug found some rocks and piled them and tree limbs around the track to protect it in case Harlan wanted to make a plaster cast of it. He then went up the mountain following the line the tracks had made to see it he could find any more clear impressions. If the horse had come down the mountain in the general direction these tracks were made then the opposite direction would be towards the canyon where the body was found. He walked, scanning the ground for sign, until he was looking down into the canyon at almost the exact spot where he had found the body. The rains had wiped out all traces and no more horse tracks could be seen.

Sitting on his haunches for a spell, he cogitated. "This is important. I need to get word to Harlan. Then again it's also obvious. We all know someone else must have been in this canyon that day. What everyone don't know is that at least one of the people here that day was riding a pony or a small horse, assuming the pony tracks were made at that time." He decided all this thinking was making his head hurt so he gave it up and went back to his tied horse. He figured he would be close to the message post tomorrow so he would leave a message for Fro to call Dub who would call Harlan.

Harlan also had plenty of time to think on his way back to La Veta. He called his wife, Celeste, to let her know he was on his way home. She worked as a teacher in the La Veta schools and was home by early afternoon. Going over everything that had transpired, he wondered whether Anita Trujillo and her brothers had anything to do with Lackey's death. Those guys could probably kill a man and not think twice about it, and maybe they did because they didn't want Lackey fooling around with their sister. They sure seemed protective of her. But if they did it, how did they get into that rough canyon? They certainly didn't ride their Harleys up there. Most likely if they wanted Lackey dead they would have completed that task in the Trinidad area. "There is something I am missing," he mused. "I've got to go back over the evidence again, or maybe there is some evidence I don't have. I've got to keep digging," he decided.

The next morning, riding a line-backed dun whose name was Dunny, Doug started out from his camp at first light, of course. Dunny was a big two-year-old gelding, just getting started in the world of cow horses. He had a lot of cow sense genetically implanted in his noggin, but he was still at that age where he could spook at a moment's notice. The wide world was pretty new to him, except that he had been raised in the mountains and was a good rock roller.

He never had offered to pitch even when first saddled. Doug gentled him last winter and he accepted the bosal and the saddle without complaint. The bosal is a halter and bridal used primarily to get young horses started. Good cowboys who are good horsemen never put bits in a young horse's mouth until they get older.

Doug and Dunny were both feeling good this particular morning. It was a cool, brisk morning with a touch of autumn in the air. "Fall will be here soon," Doug said to BC, who agreed with a wag of his tail. As they were checking some of the grassy valleys higher up around timberline they noticed that some of the cows were already drifting down toward lower country. Some of the older cows had a sixth sense about when it was time to start easing down. This was not a sudden rush, but a gradual migration to the lower, warmer country. They would graze awhile, then walk awhile. Since, in the bovine world, as well as in every other critter's world that Doug could think of, the female of the species was the leader, he wondered why the human critters usually insisted on electing males to position of leadership. Maybe this was a gradual thing, too—look how long it took women to get the right to vote.

Upon entering one of the valleys Doug noticed a gathering of magpies and ravens at the upper end back in the trees. He began riding toward this place keeping a sharp lookout for trouble. When they were still about fifty yards from the supposed kill, Dunny suddenly shied to the side, with eyes wide and nostrils flared. BC also smelled something and growled with hackles raised. Doug dismounted and led Dunny to some oak brush, tying him securely, up high, to an oak branch that was as big as his wrist. He then pulled his 30-30 from its scabbard and slowly walked toward the kill.

As he was getting closer he caught the rank odor of dead cow. BC proceeded to the kill and began his process of sniffing out the scent and determining what had happened. There was a lot of bear sign around, including several piles of bear scat, and Doug saw enough tracks to tell that it was a grizzly. It looked like the same one that had been in the area a few weeks ago. Doug was so wary of impending disaster that the hair was standing up on the back of his neck. After making sure the cow had been killed by a bear, and calling BC, he backed out of there very carefully, keeping a close watch on all his surroundings. He mounted up and they made their way to the message post where he left a note explaining everything he had found.

In the meantime, Fro was riding Sweetwater camp's ridges

and valleys, and he also noted that some of the older cows were easing down to lower country. He decided to make a big circle, check the message post, and go down to the fence line that divided the summer range from the lower country, making sure all the gates were open so the cattle could graze down unhindered. Fro had discussed this on the phone with Dub the evening before, and they decided that since it was late September they should let the cattle find their own way to lower country. Already there was snow dusting the high peaks. The fall roundup would be soon.

Fro picked up Doug's messages, noticing horse tracks around the tub, and he left a message to remind Doug to open all the gates. "If I know Doug, he's already doing that," he thought to himself. The news about the grizzly peaked his interest, and Fro wondered if he should take any special precautions to protect the cows. If the old mama cows got sight or smell of a grizzly, that would give them added incentive to head for lower, safer country.

After leaving his messages, Doug had ridden down the long valley to open the gates in the fence line. In places the valley narrowed and pinched together, and the gully had a series of dry water falls before widening out again. In these places they had to pick their way carefully around obstacles. Doug opened all the gates that were on the fence between there and his camp, noticing that some cattle were already bunched up by the fence. "The fall gather might be easy this year," he mused. Of course there were always some stragglers, and every year there usually were one or two pairs that refused to leave the summer pasture, preferring to winter in the high country if allowed.

He recalled an incident a couple of years ago when a bull and two cows with big calves had not been gathered, but were still in the high country after the fall roundup. Doug had ridden up one nice spring day and tried to get on the uphill side of them, but they saw him and high-tailed it into some heavy timber. He could not get them out, even with the help of BC. Doug and another cowboy by the name of Clyde rode back up there a few days later and when they got near the edge of a big grassy park they could see the cattle grazing with a bunch of elk on the other side of the meadow. The guys brought three good cow dogs with them this time.

They stayed in the timber and worked their way around until they were on the uphill side and upwind of the cattle. They spread out and moved down into the park. The elk stood there and looked at them, but the cattle took off running like wild animals with their tails in the air. At least they were running in the right direction. The riders and the dogs kept the cattle moving until they came to the fence and, with some difficulty, put them through a gate—all except the bull.

This was a high horned, white-faced bull, and by this time he was hot and tired. He took refuge in a large copse of oak brush. The bull had slobbers running out of his nose and mouth and was rumbling in a low, angry tone. Clyde rode his horse up close to the oak brush, yelling at the bull, trying to dislodge him. The bull was really getting pissed and came charging out of the brush, hitting Clyde's horse broadside. His horns grazed the belly of the horse, and he threw his head up and knocked the horse off its feet. Clyde managed to pull his feet out of the stirrups, but went flying and landed hard.

The bull was backing up, fixin' to make another charge, when all three dogs arrived at the same time and gave that bull a good going over. Finally, the bull decided the best thing to do was to go through the gate. Doug succeeded in getting Clyde and his horse back on their feet, only finding scrapes, bumps, and bruises. They continued driving the renegades down toward headquarters. A few days later with the help of a couple more hands, the cows were finally separated from the calves.

Dub had instructed Doug and the other hands to haul these yearling calves to headquarters and put them in a pen where they could be fattened and later butchered as beef for the ranch. But those two wild critters kept trying to go over or through the corral fence. With difficulty they finally managed to get them into a horse trailer. Doug stepped into the back of the trailer to close the middle gate when one of the steers charged him. He was knocked ass over teakettle onto the ground behind the trailer and came up covered in cow shit and dirt, cussing the day of their birth.

The men finally got both steers loaded, as well as their horses, and were making for headquarters. They were in one of the ranch's old pickup trucks and evidently the ball on the trailer hitch had significant wear on it, because as they were rolling along an old pasture road one of the cowboys looked out the driver's side window and said, "What the hell is that?" There was the trailer traveling along beside them down through the pasture. The cowboys were looking at the trailer, and the horses were looking at the cowboys, all with confused looks on their faces.

The trailer came to a barb wire fence and went right through, wires popping like banjo strings. It finally slowed down and stopped, rocking back and forth like a baby's cradle. After getting everything hooked back up they finally made it to headquarters. The only other incident was when the steers tried to jump over the fence in the fattening pen after they were unloaded. Later when Doug had a chance to enjoy smaller portions of those steers, he concluded that he had never tasted beef that good.

Harlan received a call from Dub about the pony track Doug found, and he was pondering this when he got a call from Frank Lucero at the Las Animas Sheriff's office in Trinidad.

"Harlan, this is Frank."

"Hey, Frank. How's it going?"

"Not too bad. We have been requested by the Raton sheriff's office in Colfax County, New Mexico, to bring the Trujillo brothers in for questioning. There was a liquor store hold up there a few weeks ago, and they have reason to believe the Trujillos had something to do with it. We are going to ask them politely to come into the office. If you would like to question them, too, you might want to be here."

"Yes, I want to be there when you do that. When will that happen?"

"We are hoping for tomorrow or the next day. I'll call you."

"Good. Thanks, Frank. Looking forward to seeing you soon, then," Harlan said hanging up.

He hoped he could also interview Anita Trujillo when he went to Trinidad. So, there was a possibility of someone riding a small horse or a pony in that canyon the day Lackey was murdered? Harlan couldn't imagine the Trujillo brothers riding a horse, let alone a pony. Maybe Anita, but he knew nothing about her horseback riding skills. He had to find out more about her.

Dub called Bobby Daugherty and told him the bear was back. Bobby agreed to come to the ranch as soon as possible.

"Can you get word to Doug that I will be heading up there in the next day or two? I'll go to Granger camp, since I know where it is, and I'll drive as far as I can before riding the rest of the way."

Dub said he would call Sweetwater camp and have them relay a message to Doug.

About noon two days later Bobby rode into Granger cow camp. He was leading a pack horse and had brought eight dogs—three hounds and five Airedales or Airedale crosses. Doug was not there at the time, so Bobby fed and watered his animals. He figured Doug would be back about dark-thirty, so he went into the living quarters to see what Doug had to eat. The only thing he could find was a few cans of pork and beans. "Times must be rough," Bobby mused.

He brought in his gear, including a container of green chili stew Jennifer had made and packed in his duffel. He also put together a batch of biscuits from the supplies he had brought with him. Just about the time everything was ready to eat, the hounds and Airedales set up a ruckus, barking and bawling. He stepped to the door and saw Doug riding up while BC was getting acquainted with all the dogs.

"It's about time you're getting in—supper is ready," Bobby yelled as Doug unsaddled his horse.

"I'm sorry I don't have much in the way of vittles," Doug said.

"I added a bit to your spare cupboard, so we might have enough to get by."

Doug's eyes got big when he came into the room and saw the spread. "Wow, you make a damn fine camp cook—you're hired."

"I had to bring stuff with me. A man could starve to death at this camp. You don't go grocery shopping much, do you?"

"I'll be leaving here in a few days and I didn't want to bring in stuff that I'd have to pack back out."

It was quiet for a while except for the sounds of chewing while the two men did considerable damage to the supper.

In a bit Bobby eased back from his plate and said, "I hear you're having more bear trouble?"

"Yeah, ol' Grizz is back—killed another cow, but what's exciting is I saw his track just a couple of hours ago by a pool of water not a mile from here, and it was fresh. I think we can start his trail there in the morning."

"Let's hope he makes a stand before he gets into that huge pile of rocks right on top of this mountain. I brought another fighting dog this time. I'm pitting everything I've got against him. If we don't nail him this time I may be done."

The next morning, at first light, Bobby and Doug were leading Festus the mule and all the dogs coupled together except, for Sally and BC. They didn't want to take a chance of the pack running off at the sign of just any black bear or cougar. Soon they were at the canyon where Doug had seen the grizzly track the evening before. It was a small canyon with a trickle of water in the bottom. In the sand by the edge of a small pool was the unmistakable print of a large grizzly.

Bobby dismounted and kept all the dogs with him, except for Sally who ranged both up and down the canyon until she figured out which direction the bear had gone. In about a minute she sang out in her beautiful voice down the canyon about a hundred yards. All the other dogs were getting anxious, but Bobby waited until Sally sang out a couple more times before turning two more hounds loose. Soon all three were bawling occasionally—the trail wasn't hot, but the dogs were steadily following it.

After trailing down the canyon about a mile the dogs started to climb the ridge across the canyon from where the men were. Bobby let the Airedales loose and mounted his horse. Bobby and Doug crossed the canyon and went up the other side, still within hearing of the dogs. When they topped out on the ridge the dogs were already crossing the next valley which was not so deep and much more grassy. The dogs kept trailing in the same general direction and crossed several more shallow ridges and valleys. The men could hear the dogs fine when they were up high on a ridges, but they could barely hear them when they were in the valleys.

Finally when they reached another high ridge they could hear the dogs, and it sounded like they had stopped moving and were sort of confused. Bobby and Doug continued as fast as they could to close the distance. Suddenly Sally sang out to the right from the rest of the pack, moving quickly up the side of the mountain. Before long the entire pack was voicing its opinion, strung out behind Sally. When Bobby and Doug got to the spot where the dogs had temporarily stalled they discovered a dead yearling calf that was mostly eaten.

"Looks like we disturbed his breakfast," Bobby said. "We'd better keep moving as the chase is going to get hot in a little bit."

They headed up the ridge staying on the knife edge as much as possible. The dogs were really moving fast now and angling slightly to the right toward the peak with the huge pile of rocks above timberline. The riders topped out on the ridge they were riding up, and at almost the same instant they heard the dogs' voices change. They were in full cry now, even the Airedales. This indicated the dogs could see their prey and were running with their heads up. Suddenly the sound changed again and it was obvious that a terrible fight was taking place.

The grizz was roaring and the dogs were baying. When the bear turned toward one tormenter, another Airedale or two would attack his backside. Airedales can do some damage with their teeth, but they are also extremely quick and can get out of danger when a bear turns on them. The bear would fight a while and then run up toward the mountaintop. He couldn't go any more than a few hundred yards before the dogs would catch him again, and the fight would start all over.

The terrain was getting rougher, which made it harder going for the bear as well as for the dogs. Whenever the grizz would find a bluff or rock pile to go over in hopes of escaping his tormenters, the dogs would find a way over or around it. The riders were having a hard time, too, and finally tied up their horses in a bunch of trees near timberline. They knew they were near timberline because most of the trees were corkbark—Englemann spruce—with a few bristlecone pines scattered about. Bobby and Doug collected their rifles, ropes, and anything else they thought they might need from the saddles and pack saddle. They started the arduous trek up the mountain on foot, following the dogs. Doug was having a hard time breathing and would have to stop often, trying to get a lung-full of oxygen that was scarce at that altitude.

The sound of the pack seemed to be coming from only one place now. About five hundred yards above timberline there was a huge pile of rocks with great slabs jumbled up forming large cracks and spaces underground. The grizz decided to make his stand in one of these spaces. It was about three feet wide and ten feet long with only one entrance. He had backed up in this hole and dared anything to come in after him. Some of the dogs were baying at the entrance and some were on top, sniffing and looking down into the cracks.

It took Bobby and Doug a considerable time to get to this spot, and the bear began roaring his disapproval when he caught the smell of man. Putting most of the gear down except their rifles, they began searching for a spot where they could get a bead on the bear.

> Finally Doug said, "If I get down there in front of that big boulder I think I can see back into that hole he is in."

> "The only problem is, if he comes out of there in a rush, you won't be able to get out of the way in time."

> "If he comes out I'm going to be shooting. I hope you will be, too."

Doug eased into position very carefully, keeping a close watch on the entrance to the den. There were three or four

Airedales at the entrance darting in and out and distracting the bear. When Doug got into position he could catch a glimpse of the bear when there wasn't a dog in the way. He raised and aimed his rifle hoping for a clear shot. Bobby had his rifle ready, too. Suddenly the bear charged one of the Airedales who ventured too close. The dog scrambled out of the way but the bear's head and shoulders were exposed outside of the hole. Boom! Bobby's rifle roared first, quickly followed by several shots from Doug's.

When Bobby shot, the bear had gone down with a broken left shoulder, but he quickly got back to his feet. Then one of Doug's shots hit him right between the eyes, and a shot from Bobby hit him in the left ear—two brain shots fired almost simultaneously. The bear was dead, and the dogs fell to wooling and shaking the bear in their moment of triumph. Bobby and Doug took a deep breath and spent a few moments getting over the shakes.

"I reckon he won't be killing any more cattle," Doug mused sadly.

"It's a shame, really," Bobby said. "There's not too many of these magnificent creatures left in this country. I wish none of them had to be killed."

"Here you are a professional hunter, talking like that."

"It's the truth. No one loves wildlife more than I do. I hope there are plenty still around forever. I may be a professional hunter, but I'm also a wildlife biologist—that's what my degree is—Wildlife Biology from Colorado State."

"Wow, I didn't know that. I'm impressed, and I agree with you. I love the wild, lonely places, especially when those places have plenty of wildlife," Doug said.

With their ropes they rigged a come-along and eased the bear out where they could work on it—skinning out the hide and leaving the skull intact. When Doug was skinning the chest area he found a lot of buckshot, probably from John Latham's shotgun. Some had barely penetrated the hide and had formed little balls of gristle under the skin. They didn't find any evidence of other gunshot wounds on the carcass. There were a lot of bloodshot places on all four legs, especially the hind legs and buttocks area, but those were caused by the Airedales and their ferocious teeth.

Bobby cut off some pieces of bear meat to feed the dogs, which was their reward for a job well done. What the dogs really wanted was water, and they found some in a low depression in the rocks. Bobby and Doug folded the hide and tied it to a pole so that both of them could carry it down to timberline. Their load weighed over a hundred pounds, but at least it was downhill to where the horses were tied. Festus wasn't too keen on letting them load the fresh bear hide on the pack saddle, but with a coat tied over his head he finally allowed it. It was a long, slow trip back to Granger cow camp, and they didn't arrive until late afternoon.

Harlan received a phone call from Frank Lucero and started for Trinidad. There was plenty of time to recall the details of the case while making the drive. He had subpoenaed phone records from Lackey's phone, Jim Rice's phone, and the Trujillos, but he had not found anything of interest. It was evident that Lackey's wife was having an affair with Jim Rice, but they certainly didn't talk much by phone. Likewise, there were no calls between the Trujillos and Lackey. Harlan mused about the pony track Doug had found, wondering if there was a connection between it and the murder. Dub said that Doug seemed confident they were made around the same time.

Upon arriving at the Trinidad sheriff's office Harlan waited while the Trujillo brothers were brought into separate interrogation rooms. The youngest one, who was about eighteen or nineteen, was in handcuffs. Harlan observed the proceedings through the one-way glass. Frank asked a lot of questions as to their whereabouts on certain dates. The two deputies from New Mexico asked a lot of questions about the time of the liquor store holdup in Raton. The two youngest brothers refused to answer any questions. The oldest answered a few questions with an "I don't know what you're talking about," or "I don't remember." It was apparent they had been through this before and knew the routine.

Frank finally came out of the interview room and asked Harlan if he wanted to ask some questions. Harlan and Frank went back into the room together.

> The oldest brother gave Harlan a look of recognition and said, "Well, if it isn't ol' Huerfano County!"
>
> "Yeah, I missed you too," Harlan said sarcastically. "So I hear you have been up to no good over in Raton."
>
> There was no comment, so he continued. "Do you know a man by the name of Jim Lackey?"
>
> "No, who the hell is he?"
>
> "He's the guy that's been screwing your sister. You should know him."

A look of hatred came into Trujillo's eyes and he tensed up but did not say anything.

> "I think you knew he was having it on with your sister and you killed him. I just hope I can pin this on you boys before the New Mexico deputies take you away."
>
> "Are you talking about that old guy at the cantina who kept trying to buy Anita a beer?"
>
> "Oh, he paid Anita for a lot more than beer. I even know which motel they were going to."

Trujillo lunged over the table toward Harlan, his anger raging, when a deputy grabbed him and shoved him back down. "Anita would never have anything to do with that gringo piece of crap," he roared.

"So did you kill him?" Harlan asked.

"No, but if I knew he was messing with Anita, I would have," Trujillo answered, trying to regain his composure.

Harlan ended his interview and left the room. It appeared that the New Mexico investigators had a witness who recognized the Harleys and they had a fairly good case against the Trujillo brothers. Whether it was enough for an arrest or not, Harlan didn't know and didn't stay long to find out. After saying his good-byes to Frank, Harlan went again to the cantina in hopes of finding Anita there. When he arrived, a pretty young Latina was parking a fairly new pickup in the parking lot. It was one of the trucks Harlan had seen in the Trujillos' front yard when he had been to their place. Harlan waited at the front door for the girl.

When she stepped closer, she smiled, looking at Harlan's handsome face and his muscular arms and shoulders. "Hi," she said coyly. She was a young-looking eighteen-year-old with long dark hair, a trim figure, wearing a pretty white blouse that revealed plenty of cleavage. The white of the blouse contrasted beautifully with her lovely olive skin. Her skirt was light blue and cut very short. She wore white go-go boots that accented her legs. Harlan knew why this cantina had so many male patrons, both young and old.

"Hello there," Harlan said with a smile. "Are you Anita Trujillo?"

"Yes, I am." Her smile changed slightly. "Who—oh, now I know—you were at my house a while ago."

"Yes, I was. I just wanted to talk to you, but your brothers wouldn't allow it. I'm Harlan Martinez, deputy sheriff from Huerfano County." He showed her his badge.

"Yeah, they can be overprotective at times. If I had

known how handsome you are, I would have let you in," she replied with the bright smile again.

"I have a few questions for you about a case I'm working on. Would you like to talk here or somewhere else?"

"Let's go inside. I might as well answer questions while I'm on the clock."

As they entered the cantina a roar of approval rose up from all the male patrons. After clocking in and being admonished by Rosa for being a couple minutes late, Anita joined Harlan at the bar.

"What do you want to know?" she asked.

"Do you know this man?" Harlan asked, showing the picture of Lackey.

"Yes, he is an acquaintance that I met here. He comes in about every month or six weeks."

"Anita, I should warn you, I have done considerable investigating and I already know the answer to a lot of these questions, so please don't lie to me."

Her black eyes looked intently into his, not so much smiling now, but with a harder glint in them.

"Okay, mister handsome lawman, I know him. He buys me things...he treats me like I'm his baby doll...he helped me buy that pickup out there, so I'm nice to him. Is that against the law? I'm not a whore if that's what you're thinking."

"No, I never suggested that. I'm just trying to find out what happened to him."

"Why, has something happened to Jim?"

"I'm sorry to tell you his body was found in the mountains. It appears that someone shot him."

A look of horror came over her and her face paled. She staggered against Harlan and he helped her into a chair.

"What...what...who...why?" she asked visibly shaken.

"We don't know yet. That's why I'm here. I need to know if anyone had a grudge or hated him badly enough to want him dead."

"I don't know anything about that. I loved him in a way. I mean, he was always so sweet to me," she answered visibly upset.

"How about your brothers? They seem to resent anyone who shows an interest in you."

"They don't own me. I do what I want," she scoffed. "Where did you say this happened?"

"In some pretty rough country high in the mountains, around June the 20th."

"Then it would be impossible for them to do it. They would never go anywhere that can't be reached with their damn bikes. In June I was wondering what happened to Jim. I even called his house, but his bitch of a wife answered the phone and she wouldn't tell me anything. I thought maybe he got another girlfriend. Mike told me," she nodded her head toward the bartender, "Jim was flirting with another woman in here one time. Jim always thought he was a dandy with the women."

"Anita, are you going to work today or what?" Rosa barked, approaching the table. "Why are you so pale? What have you done to her?" she scowled at Harlan.

"I'll be okay. I'm going to work now. Jim is dead!" Anita said in disbelief looking at Rosa.

"Forget about him, sweetie," Rosa said, giving the girl a hug. "The world is full of men, and you need to hold out for a good one that deserves you."

"Just a couple more questions," Harlan said to Anita, "Do you ride horses and have you ever ridden in the mountains?"

"Horses?" she answered in surprise, "No, I don't, and in fact they scare me. I never rode a horse in my life."

"Mike told me that Lackey was trying to put the move on another girl who was in here one time, but her boyfriend put a stop to it. Do you know anything about that incident?"

"All I know is that when I arrived in the parking lot and was coming into the cantina, I saw a girl and a guy leaving. I remember she was pretty and they were getting into a red truck. I remembered it because Mike told me Jim was trying to put the moves on that girl. Mike doesn't like Jim much. I asked Jim about it and, of course, he denied everything."

"If you can think of anything that might help, call me," Harlan said, handing her one of his business cards.

"I just might do that. Are you married?" she asked weakly.

"Yes, I am. Very much so."

"Too bad," she said sadly, going off to wait on tables.

As Harlan was driving home and thinking about the day's

events, he decided that the girl was either innocent or a very good actress. She seemed like a sweet kid, despite her family, but he reminded himself not to be turned by a pretty face. He just couldn't make himself believe that the Trujillo brothers were up in that rough country.

"This case is a stinker. There is something I'm not seeing. Rice would be a more logical candidate. I've got to pin down where he was on the twentieth of June."

Arriving home late that night, he was met with a cool reception from his lovely wife, Celeste. She was a very beautiful woman in her late twenties. When she wore heels she was as tall as Harlan, who was six foot in height. Celeste's hair was as black as a raven's wing and longer than shoulder length. She had the unusual attribute, for a Latina, of having the most beautiful hazel eyes Harlan had ever seen. They met at Colorado State University, fell in love, and shared a room until they graduated. She received her degree in education, and his was in law enforcement. They were married right after graduation and settled in La Veta when he was hired by the sheriff's department and she by the La Veta schools as a teacher.

Whenever he came home from work, or saw her again after several hours' absence, it made his heart sing. He was so proud of her and of being married to her that it made his shirt buttons pop.

"Where have you been, mister—it's getting late?" she questioned.

"You knew I was going to Trinidad today. I was interviewing a very pretty Latina girl, that's why I'm so late."

"You have a Latina girl here to interview—you don't have to look anywhere else," Celeste said teasingly while snuggling into his arms.

After they did a little smooching she asked, "Are you hungry? I've put the kids to bed. You can go say good night while I heat up your supper."

Harlan visited the children's bedrooms—a boy, age six, and a girl, age eight, giving them each a kiss before rejoining Celeste in the kitchen.

Doug was kept very busy moving all the cattle down towards lower country. Now that he didn't have a grizzly to worry about, he could concentrate on the cow business. He checked all the areas that had good grass, the valleys and some of the ridges. He never failed to find cattle there, and he and BC would gather and drive them until they were all moving along fairly well on their own. Then they would go look for some more.

He found out from the message post that Bobby had left the grizzly hide with Dub when he got paid, and Dub decided to get it made into a bear rug to mount on a wall in the main house at headquarters.

One weekend when they were not in school, Dub sent a couple of teenagers up to Granger camp to help gather cows and herd them out of the high country. These young men were riding beside each other one day behind a bunch of cows and calves that had been gathered off a long ridge. They were out of hearing of Doug's voice and assumed there was no cause for alarm. They were dawdling along talking about their favorite subject—girls—and not paying too much attention to what they were doing.

One of them said, "I noticed you still have that spotting scope in your room at the bunkhouse. Are you still looking at that lady in the house down the hill?"

"Yeah, she sure is pretty. I keep hoping that I will see her naked sometime, but she closes the curtains when she gets ready for bed."

"Man, she is way too old for you."

"Yeah, but a guy can dream can't he?"

"Are you going to leave your stuff at the bunkhouse or take it home?"

"I'm going to leave it there for a while. Dub said we could work on weekends as much as we wanted, at least through fall roundup."

Doug yelled, "Hey, you guys! You're letting some cattle get away," sending BC after the strays. "I wonder if these kids are a help or a nuisance," Doug muttered to himself.

After a couple weeks of searching and gathering, Doug and Fro were confident they had pushed all the cattle out of the mountains. They had occasional help from other cowhands but did the majority of the work themselves, with the aid of their trusty cow dogs. On the last day at his camp, Doug packed everything on Festus and Big Red. He was mounted on Frog Honey and driving all his horses in front of him as they headed down the mountain. It was a very brisk morning with the temperature below freezing. Ice was forming on the edges of the little pond in front of the line shack. It was an uneventful trip as all the horses knew where they were headed. Thoughts of a warm barn and plenty of grain at headquarters occupied their brains.

When the entourage arrived at headquarters, Doug got all the horses settled in and fed. He stowed the pack saddles at either the saddle barn or with his personal stuff at the bunkhouse. When he entered the bunkhouse he found that his old room was occupied by someone else's belongings. He noticed a spotting scope near the window and looked to see where it was aimed. Through the scope he could see the back of one of the rental houses the ranch owned. "I wonder what that is all about?" he mused.

Harlan got in touch with the Colorado Livestock Board in Denver and asked if each livestock inspector worked according to a strict schedule and was assigned jobs, or whether they worked independently. He was told that it worked both ways. Sometimes customers would call the individual inspector, and sometimes they would schedule visits through the main office. Individual inspectors were supposed to keep the main office informed at all times of their whereabouts, but this rule was not always followed.

Harlan tried to determine Jim Rice's whereabouts on or about the twentieth of June, and was told that it looked like he was working in and around Alamosa. Harlan received the list of the customers who had cattle inspected during that time. Next, he made phone calls to each one, recording the times and dates that people gave him. Some couldn't remember the times exactly. In trying to piece together the time line, there seemed to be enough gaps to raise doubt about Jim's alibi. Harlan had little time for homicide detecting, though, because all his other duties took up about ninety percent of his time.

When Doug got all his chores done and was finished with supper at the cookhouse, he retired to the bunkhouse. The two young cowboys were already in the room, which had been Doug's room last winter.

"What are you two up to?" Doug asked as he came into the room.

"Oh, we're just hanging out," one of them replied.

"How come you're in my room?"

"We didn't know it was your room when we moved in. We can move into another room if you want us to."

"No, that's okay. I'll put my possibles in one of the other rooms."

"What's that—*possibles?*" one of the youngsters asked.

"That's what a cowboy calls his belongings, and he always has a *possibles* bag to carry things. There could be possibly anything in that bag," Doug said laughing. "I've got a question for you fellers. If you see three men in the front seat of a ranch pickup, can you tell which one is the real cowboy just by where he sits?"

"Well, there isn't any way to tell," one of them answered.

"Sure there is," Doug said. "It's the fellow in the middle. Number one, he don't have to drive. Number two, he has full control of the radio. And number three, he don't have to open and shut the gates."

They had a good laugh, and then Doug asked, "What is that spotting scope used for? You looking for elk?"

They both looked a little sheepish, and finally the one who owned the scope said, "I brought it to the ranch in hopes of spotting some elk. Then one evening I was looking around with it and I saw this house down there, just off the road that leads to town. As I was looking I noticed a very pretty lady lives there, so I started watching her. She must be single because I've never seen anyone else there."

"You're a peeping tom?" Doug asked in surprise.

"He's also a sex maniac," the other young lad added. "He watches her hoping he'll see her naked."

"Shut up!" the peeper retorted, obviously embarrassed.

"So have you seen her naked yet?" asked Doug.

"No, but I got to watch her ride her horse."

"She has a horse?" Doug asked surprised.

"Yeah, some days when she gets home from work she goes for a ride back in those hills," he said pointing east.

"What kind of horse?"

"It looks like a small paint mare, although I've never seen it up close."

"That is very interesting," Doug answered thoughtfully. "So you all haven't seen anyone else there?"

"No. One time I saw another vehicle there but didn't see who was driving it."

"When was this, and can you describe the vehicle?"

"It was probably back in June, because it wasn't too long after we started here for the summer. The pickup was a red four-wheel-drive. I don't know the make."

"How long was it there?" Doug asked.

"Just for a weekend, and I haven't seen it since," the teenager answered.

Doug was amazed they could remember as much as they did, since most teenagers seemed to have Attention Deficit Disorder—at least most of them that he had any dealings with.

When Harlan finally was able to get back to his desk and devote some time to the case, after trying to keep up with his many other duties, he decided he needed to go to Alamosa and talk face-to-face with some of the ranchers. He called his boss, Sheriff Sisneros, and got permission to make the trip. After arranging some meetings with the people that lived in and around Alamosa, he scheduled a time to interview each of them. A couple of days later he went to Alamosa to keep his appointments.

The first was with a rancher who had received cattle to put out on grass for the summer. Rice, who was filling in for another inspector at the time, had checked these same cattle and gave the rancher a copy of the inspection sheet. Harlan was able to establish an exact time line for Rice's visit to this ranch. Next he visited a packer who had several steers he was going to butcher, and again a definite time line was established.

The third customer was a rancher and his wife who had gathered a bunch of yearlings and wanted to ship them to a ranch in New Mexico for the summer. When he arrived at this ranch a woman answered the door who was quite pretty. She was probably about fifty and had the trim figure most woman have who work out of doors a lot and who spend a lot of time in the saddle. She was about five-eight with blond hair, blue eyes, wearing blue jeans and a denim shirt that she filled out very nicely.

"Sheriff Martinez, I assume?" she asked, giving Harlan the once over with her eyes.

"Yes, ma'am, only I'm a deputy," he said, showing his shield. "I need to talk to you and your husband if I may."

"I'm Linda Olsen," she extended her hand. "My husband, Bill, is out working cattle at the moment but should be home before too long. I would normally be helping him except one of us had to be here to talk to you."

"I'm sorry to take you away from your work. You can probably answer any questions I have. I will try to make this as quick as possible."

"Take your time. I'm not going anywhere today."

"Back in June you shipped some cattle and had a livestock inspector by the name of Jim Rice check them. Do you remember that?"

Her eye brows rose slightly and a faint look of surprise crossed her face when he mentioned Jim's name.

"Yes, I remember it very well. As I told you on the phone, he was definitely here. Jim is a good looking young man, and I'm not likely to forget him."

"Did he give you a receipt for the inspection that he completed?"

"Why do you need that? Is Jim in some kind of trouble?"

"I'm investigating a murder and I have to follow up on all kinds of leads. I'm just trying to tie up some loose ends."

"Jim would never have anything to do with something like that," she exclaimed.

"You seem to know him purty well. Have you had a lot of dealings with Jim?"

"Well," she smiled, "I'm just a good judge of character, having dealt with a lot of men in my lifetime. I know in my heart that Jim is a good man."

She went to a desk that was in a corner of the kitchen and rifled through a bunch of papers, coming up with the inspection report. She handed it to Harlan and he checked the information on the report, writing some notes on his pad.

"Everything seems to be in order, ma'am. I will get out of your hair."

"There is no rush. Would you like some coffee? I have some made—and please call me Linda."

"That would be very nice, thank you." Harlan got the impression that Mrs. Olsen was probably lonely and enjoyed having company.

As they were sitting at the kitchen table, enjoying their coffee, she offered, "I can assure you those dates and times are authentic. I remember very well when he was here. In fact, I'm not likely to forget."

"Why is that, Linda?" Harlan's interest was piqued.

"Can I trust you?"

"Of course. If it pertains to this case, however, I have an obligation to provide information for the court."

"I wouldn't want Bill to know. You see my husband hasn't been able to raise a flag in years, and Jim gave me something I really needed. So I can certainly vouch for his whereabouts for a couple of hours the day he was here."

"Well, I think I have all the information I need," Harlan said, slightly embarrassed and getting up to leave. "I want to thank you for being so candid."

"You're quite welcome. I hope you're not one for idle gossip?" she asked anxiously.

"Not to worry. I am not allowed to gossip about information I obtain during an interview. It's like with a lawyer—it's privileged," he explained as they were walking out to his unit. "Once again, thank you very much."

"You're quite welcome," she said, waving goodbye.

One evening, after a full day of rounding up cattle, Doug decided to take a walk after supper. He strolled out behind the bunkhouse and down the slight slope toward the road. Soon he was on the back side of the horse trap next to the rental house where the young lady lived. There was a gate on the back fence with horse tracks and evidence of recent use. Upon examining the tracks he was almost positive it was the same track he had seen up on the mountain. It was a small track, almost pony size.

He walked to the small barn that was behind the house, and inside was a paint mare a little larger than a pony. The mare was eating some grain from the trough on the side of the barn, and there was some hay in the rack above the trough. Doug talked gently to the mare and petted her before easing down to pick up a front foot. He was examining the foot when a voice behind him demanded,

"What are you doing to my horse?"

Doug was startled, for he hadn't heard anyone approach.

"Sorry, ma'am, I was just checking the shoe. I saw the

tracks out there," waving toward the area behind the horse trap, "and thought it looked like a loose shoe."

"Well, is it loose?" She was tall for a woman, maybe five-ten, with long brown hair, slender in build, but with a very good figure and a strikingly beautiful face.

"No, it's fine. My name is Doug Jepsen and I work on this ranch. You're the lady that came to the cookhouse one day asking about a lost ferret," he said, extending his hand.

She still hadn't got over her irritation, and she ignored his hand. "Yes, did you ever find it?"

"No, ma'am. I'm sorry that I disturbed you. Please be assured I didn't mean to upset you."

"If the shoe was loose I would have noticed it. I'm not a novice around horses."

"Did you grow up around horses?"

"Yes, I did."

"Where was that, ma'am?"

"What's with all the questions? I don't even know you."

"Sorry, ma'am. Like I said, I'm Doug Jepsen. Your name is?"

She studied him for a moment with a look of suspicion in her eyes. "I'm Angela Ransom," she said, finally taking his extended hand.

"We've been neighbors for a while. I'm glad we finally met," Doug said. "I'll get out of your hair, Angela, and

I'm sorry to have bothered you."

"I guess your intentions were honorable." She stepped back letting him leave the small paddock.

"It is my pleasure to finally meet you," Doug said, "Maybe I'll see you again sometime."

"Possibly. After all, like you said, we are neighbors."

"It's probably none of my business, but are you married or have a significant other?"

"You're right. It's none of your business," she answered.

Doug quietly retraced his steps up to the bunkhouse. It had been a curious meeting, but he had to get some sleep before rolling out for work at first light.

The fall roundup was in full swing. Cowboys would gather a bunch of cows and calves, usually about two to three hundred head. They would then drive them into a set of working pens where they could sort and separate them. The calves were taken away from their mothers and herded into a pasture of their own, the cows going to another pasture nearby. If any of the calves needed branding or castrating that was accomplished as well. There was always a lot of bawling by both mother cows and calves after this separation took place.

Dub would look over the calves and pick out a few heifers that he thought would make good replacement stock. Then he would cut out some of the old cows, especially if they were dry or didn't have any grazing teeth left. The old cows went into another pen from which they would be shipped to a cattle buyer. The young heifers would be kept separate, especially from the bulls, until they were at least two years old.

One day when they had finished a little earlier than usual, Doug decided to go to town and do some shopping. His old

Levis and shirts were getting a bit threadbare, and he also needed other things like shaving gear. Usually he had Dub's wife Polly pick up what he needed when she went to town, but on this particular day he decided to go himself. He fired up his old brown Ford pickup and after it coughed and sputtered a while they finally got lined out for town. As he was pulling into the outskirts of La Veta he recognized a sheriff's vehicle on the side of the road. He pulled up to it, driver's side door to driver's side door. It was Harlan on traffic patrol.

"Hey, cowboy. I haven't seen you in a while," Harlan greeted Doug.

"I know, it's been a while. So I assume you and your fat friends made it out of the mountains okay with that body," Doug teased.

"Yeah, those ol' boys aren't used to that kind of activity."

"How are Celeste and the kids? Everyone okay?"

"Everyone is fine. I'll tell them I saw you."

"Have you solved the case yet? I haven't heard anything. I just got out of the mountains about a week or so ago."

"No, I've followed up on several leads, but nothing definite yet. I heard that you found some horse tracks up on the mountain."

"Yeah, I preserved them for you. They were either a pony or a small horse, and the tracks were made about the same time Lackey was killed. I backtracked them and they led me to the canyon where I had found him."

"That is very interesting. Do you know the horse that made the tracks?"

"Well, I didn't before, but I do now. I saw that horse just a few days ago. It's a small paint mare that belongs to a girl by the name of Angela Ransom who is renting a house on the ranch."

"Wait a minute. Doesn't she work at the library here in town?"

"I don't know where she works."

"What does she look like?"

"She is tall, slender, with long brown hair and very cute."

"Yeah, that's her. She works at the town library and is friends with Celeste, I think. Did you ask her what she was doing up in the mountains back in June?" Harlan asked.

"Our conversation never got that far. She was very cool to me when she caught me examining her horse's feet and was suspicious. Also, those sex starved teenagers that have been working on the ranch during the summer told me something interesting."

"What was that?"

"One of them had a spotting scope and was watching wildlife, only not all deer and elk. He was watching that girl when she was home. They told me they saw a red four-wheel-drive pickup parked there at her house one weekend."

"Did they say who was driving it?"

"No, they never saw it arrive or leave. And they didn't know the make."

"Are you sure it was her horse that made the tracks?"

"Harlan! Of course I'm sure. I know every horse in this part of the county by its tracks."

Harlan knew that was true. Every horse makes a distinctive foot imprint, and an experienced cowboy like Doug could recognize them when he saw them.

"I probably need to interview that girl, but how do I do that without spooking her?"

"I don't know, Mr. Detective. I suggest you find out more about her. Where did she come from, what's her story, things like that?"

"Yeah, I'll do that," Harlan said. "Join me for a beer later?"

"Sure, I've got some shopping to do but I'll meet you at the Ranch Bar later," Doug answered.

When Doug had gone Harlan called the main dispatcher at the Walsenburg sheriff's office, telling her the information he needed with instructions to call him by phone when they had any results. Then he headed back to his office in La Veta to finish some paperwork. He was about to leave the office when the phone rang. One of the Walsenburg deputies had been busy searching the public records for a person named Angela Ransom. What was discovered was very interesting.

Harlan then called his wife, Celeste, to tell her he was going to join Doug for a beer at the Ranch Bar, asking her if she wanted to join them. Also, he asked her if she knew the lady who worked at the library and what she knew about her. In a few minutes all three of them arrived at the bar at about the same time. They said their greetings and sat in a booth near the back, ordering three beers. Celeste explained that she knew Angela because she frequented the library, mainly with her students. She and Angela were acquainted, but not close friends.

"Did she ever mention where she came from?" Harlan asked.

"No, and I never pried. I have no idea where she came from. She seems to be well educated, though. She doesn't have an accent in her speech that would be identifiable," Celeste answered.

"Do you have any other evidence that indicates who might have been involved in Lackey's murder?" Doug asked.

"As you know I'm not allowed to discuss a case while it's being worked. All I can say is every lead I've had so far has gone nowhere," Harlan said.

"So, the most promising lead so far is a single pony track made by a lady's horse, and we know nothing about the lady."

"I might be able to add something to that without revealing too much, but you two have to promise me not to spread this around," Harlan said.

"What's that?" both Celeste and Doug asked, giving their promise.

"The sheriff's office searched the public records and came up with a driver's license and public utility records for the last two years, but not much else," Harlan whispered.

"How does that add anything? Looks like you have zilch," Doug mused.

"How does someone live to be, what, thirty, and not have any public record?"

Suddenly a light came on and Celeste offered, "Maybe before moving here she never existed, at least as Angela Ransom."

"Exactly!" Harlan said.

"Wow, this is bizarre," Doug offered. "There is something else to consider. Whoever turned Lackey's horse loose, knows something about horses and cares about them. They took the bridle off and tied it on the saddle so that it wouldn't get tangled and so the horse could graze and would not step on the reins. The cinch was loosened slightly. I'm just saying it's possible that whoever killed Lackey knows horses, like a cowboy or someone like Angela Ransom who claims to know horses.

"The trick is how to interview her without spooking her. If she is involved, she is not alone. I'd bet she has a boyfriend who drives a red pickup. So both of you keep this information under your hat until I can sort it out. Celeste, we need to go get the kids."

They finished their beers and made their way out of the bar, saying their good-byes and agreeing to meet soon and go dancing.

Before heading back to the ranch Doug decided to visit John Latham, who lived on a small ranchette with his family on the outskirts of La Veta. They had a three bedroom one-level house with attached garage and a small barn and corral out back. Their livestock consisted of two horses, a milk cow, and various other animals including chickens and pets. They had an old tan Ford pickup with stock racks on the back, as well as a blue sedan that Sonja drove to work as a cook at the school cafeteria. John was a day-worker on various ranches in the area, and usually worked all summer for the Circle Cross at the Sweetwater line camp. Both vehicles were parked in the yard when Doug drove in, as it was late evening and everyone seemed to be home.

Doug was greeted at the door with hugs and squeals of delight from the girls and a handshake from Albert. John was sitting in a recliner with his feet propped up and a pair of crutches within reach. His left leg was in a cast from his hip to his toes. Sonja came into the living room from the kitchen where she was preparing supper and greeted Doug.

"Hi Doug. It's good to see you again. How are you?"

"I'm fine, but how are you doing?" he asked, looking over at John.

"I'm much better now. That bear business up in the mountains scared me to death."

"It scared me too. You don't have to worry about that bear anymore—we got him."

"Good!" Sonja exclaimed. "It almost killed my husband and tried to kill all of us. I hate to see any living creature killed, but that thing was evil. Thanks for coming by Doug. He needs a pick-me-up," nodding her head toward John. "Come on kids I could use some help in the kitchen," and they all hustled out of the living room.

"How you doin' John?" Doug asked, setting down on the sofa near John's chair.

"I'm doing fine—just getting damn tired of sitting," John answered agitated.

He had four angry red scars across the left side of his face running from his forehead down to his chin. The scars continued down on his chest and were visible at the vee in his shirt.

"Are you able to get up and do anything?"

"Yeah, with the help of these sticks," indicating the crutches. "I can go out and do chores somewhat. I go to physical therapy once a week and to the doctor about once a month, but mostly now it's just waiting to get everything healed up. I'm getting damn tired of sitting here and watching soap operas on TV, though."

"What's the prognosis? You gonna to be able to ride again?"

"That remains to be seen. The worst thing is my left leg. The bone was crushed right above the knee and so far I can't bend it. The doctors operated on it a couple of times trying to get everything pieced back together. The scars from the operation and where the bear bit me itch like crazy under the cast. They've taken the cast off three times already and put on new ones. The physical therapy people are working on the leg, when the cast is off, trying to get it to bend, and hopefully we'll be successful. I may have to have a knee replacement before it's all over. I had some broken ribs but they are healing fine now."

"Just think of all the mileage you'll get out of all of this. The way you like to tell bullshit stories—this one could last you the rest of your life!" Doug joked.

"Now wait a minute. You know I never tell a tale that ain't the truth." John smiled.

"Is the insurance paying for everything? Do you all need anything?" Doug asked concerned.

"The insurance is paying for everything so far, that and workman's comp. Dub paid me for a full summers' work, so that helped. We can still buy beans, so we're doing okay. Sonja and the kids have been real troopers through all of this, so I guess I'm really blessed. It's hard not to feel sorry for myself, sometimes, and I really feel bad that you and Fro and the rest of the hands had to do all my work."

"Yeah I feel pretty bad about that too," Doug said jokingly, "but we managed somehow. The fall roundup is coming along and things should slow down before too long. We still have to ship, but most of the heavy work is done."

"Supper's ready," Sonja sang out, coming into the room and wiping her hands on a dish towel. "Doug, you are staying for supper?"

"My timing is impeccable," Doug said, helping John to his crutches and to the kitchen.

A day or two later Harlan stopped by the public library and was browsing through some books when a pretty brunette approached. She was tall, as tall as Celeste, and had a nice smile. "May I help you, sir?"

"I was just looking around for something to read. My wife, Celeste, suggested I come here and see what you have available."

"We have quite a variety of books. Not a lot of them, but a good selection for a small town library, I think."

"Yeah, I'm sure I can find something. I like these Louie L'Amour books."

"Good choice. Did I hear you say your wife's name is Celeste? Is she a teacher?"

"Yes," Harlan said, feigning surprise, "Do you know her?"

"Yes, she comes in with the school children sometimes. Sweet person."

"Yes, she is—she must be to put up with me," he said smiling. "My name is Harlan Martinez. I'm the representative from the sheriff's office assigned to this area."

"Angela Ransom," she held out her hand.

"Pleased to make your acquaintance," Harlan said, taking her hand. "So are you from this area? I don't think I know any Ransom's in these parts."

Her smile faded and she hesitated before answering, "No, I was raised in Kansas. I don't have any family here."

"Oh, yeah, what part of Kansas?" Harlan asked.

"I'm sorry, but I have some other customers." She went over to where other people were looking at books.

Harlan checked out a Louis L'Amour novel and when he got outside he noticed a mini-pickup parked in the reserved parking space marked "Staff." He memorized the license plate number.

One morning a few days later Doug was loading salt and mineral blocks onto one of the ranch's Power Wagons when he noticed a mini-pickup pull into the area where the dumpsters were kept. The salt shed, the cottonseed cake storage bin, and the dumpsters were all along the main road to allow easy access for the delivery trucks and the garbage hauler. He noticed Angela get out of the mini-pickup, throw a bag of trash into one of the dumpsters, get back into her vehicle, and drive off.

Doug finished loading the salt and mineral to fill the tubs that are scattered throughout the winter pastures. As he pulled out of the yard he took a little detour and drove over to the dumpsters. He found the bag that Angela just tossed and he retrieved it. He then drove to ranch headquarters, which was Dub and Polly's house, and using their phone called Harlan's office. Luckily the deputy was in, and when he told Harlan what he had, Harlan asked him to keep the bag with him and he would meet Doug later at ranch headquarters.

Later that afternoon after Doug made his rounds to fill

the salt tubs, he met Harlan at Dub's house. Doug carried the bag of trash over to Harlan's unit, placing it on his tailgate. Harlan put on some disposable gloves and retrieved several evidence bags from his vehicle before undoing the twist-tie and opening the bag. The first thing he pulled out was a water bottle. Holding it by the bottom, he examined the top and noticed some lipstick.

"I think the lab boys can get fingerprints from this," he said, putting the bottle in an evidence bag. "I'll take all of this and see what else we can come up with."

They made arrangements to meet the following weekend at a honky-tonk in Cuchara, a small village south of La Veta where there was going to be a country western dance, complete with a live band.

Doug was kept busy the rest of the week, shipping yearlings and old cows, and keeping up with the endless list of chores that come up on a busy ranch. On Saturday he quit work early, shaved and showered, put on his new Levis and a new western shirt, a fairly new hat, and headed out for the dance. Cuchara is a small town about twenty five miles south of La Veta, nestled in a mountain pass with the Spanish Peaks to the east and the Sangre de Cristo mountains to the west.

The Cuchara Bar and Grill had a lounge area large enough for a few tables and chairs, as well as a dance floor with space for a band. About once a month they booked a musical group, and a lot of the ranchers, cowboys, and cowgirls would gather to dance, visit, and have a couple of beers. The band on this particular evening was Bill and Bonnie. Bonnie played the piano and sang, while Bill played lead guitar and did vocals. They were accompanied by a bass player who provided harmonies. Once in a while Bill would pick up the fiddle and play that for a spell.

Shortly after Doug arrived and procured a table, Celeste and Harlan came in to join him. After exchanging greetings they ordered beers.

Doug asked, "Did you get that bag of trash sent off to the lab boys?"

"I sure did. The sheriff's office sent it to the state crime lab. It will take them a while to get it processed," Harlan answered.

About that time a bunch of people arrived who worked at the Boy Scout and Girl Scout camps in the National Forest nearby. Among this group was a girl who was cute as a spotted pup in a red coaster wagon. She was in her late twenties or early thirties, wearing a very pretty "hippie" dress. She was about five-eight with short light brown hair, and a cute turned up freckled nose. As soon as Doug saw this girl he was bowled over. Celeste, who had ask Doug a question, looked at him when he didn't answer. Doug was staring at the girl in awe with his mouth hanging open.

"Doug... Doug, did you hear me?" Celeste asked.

Doug finally came to and said, "I'm sorry, I must have been distracted. Would you excuse me for a minute."

He got up and walked over to the girl and asked if she would like to dance.

"Did you see that?" Celeste asked Harlan.

"Yes, I did. What happened to him—he looked like he'd been pole-axed," Harlan responded.

"I think he finally saw a girl that he is attracted to. I was beginning to wonder about him. He has carried a broken heart way too long. We might as well dance, too."

The band was playing a good western two-step and the

dancers were moving around the dance floor when Harlan said, "Well, I'll be. Look who just walked in." He nodded toward the entrance, and there was Angela accompanied by a tall good looking cowboy dressed in jeans, a red western shirt, and wearing a white cowboy hat that was pushed back on his head with a shock of red hair sticking out in front. Angela was wearing a denim skirt, cowgirl boots, and a red and white blouse, under a denim jacket. She and her cowboy friend looked around for an empty table, but all of them either had people sitting at them or beers on the table to indicate they were occupied.

Harlan and Celeste moved over toward them saying, "Hello. Good to see you again. You can sit at our table, if you want."

As soon as Angela saw them, her smile faded and she paled slightly. "Thanks, but I don't think we are staying," she said.

"Hi, I'm Harlan Martinez," Harlan said sticking his hand out to the cowboy.

"Sully," the cowboy answered shaking Harlan's hand. "We might as well have one dance before we go," he said to Angela, guiding her out onto the dance floor.

"Wait here," Harlan said to Celeste, "and if they make a move to leave, come outside and whistle."

Harlan went out to the parking lot and began looking at the vehicles parked there. There were a lot of pickups, but finally on the end of the parking lot he found a red Chevrolet four-wheel-drive pickup with Las Animas County plates. He copied down the number and headed in, sitting down at their table just before the song ended. As he leaned back in his chair he noticed that Angela and Sully went out the front door.

Celeste joined him at the table, followed by Doug with a girl in tow.

"I want you guys to meet Rita. She is here with some friends that work at the Scout camp. Rita, these are my good friends Celeste and Harlan Martinez."

They shook hands all around and sat down to order another round of beers.

"Are you from around here, Rita?" Celeste asked.

"No, I was raised in Guymon, Oklahoma, but I went to university at Eastern New Mexico and after graduating came out to the mountains. I've always loved the high country ever since I was little. My family would go on summer vacation to the mountains of New Mexico, and I worked at the Bear Mountain Scout Ranch for a couple of years before coming up to Colorado."

"Do you like that kind of work?"

"Yes," she said, looking at Doug and smiling. "You get to meet some of the nicest people."

Doug was grinning from ear to ear.

"Did you see them?" Harlan asked Doug.

"Who?"

"Angela and her boyfriend were in here a few minutes ago."

"You're kidding. I guess I haven't noticed anyone else," Doug said sheepishly, glancing at Rita.

"Anyway, now I have another lead to work on."

"Lead?" Rita questioned.

"Harlan is a deputy sheriff, and even though he doesn't have his uniform on now, he can't stop being a cop," Doug explained.

"I've been working on a case and a person of interest was in here a while ago," Harlan said.

About this time the band started playing again and everyone got up to dance. As the evening was coming to an end and everyone was getting ready to leave, Rita informed the friends she had come with that she would ride home with Doug. They looked like two love birds when they left in Doug's pickup.

After Harlan got to work on Monday morning he had the sheriff's office run the plates on the red pickup he saw Saturday night. They called back in a short while and told him that the plates belong to a Chevrolet pickup owned by a Sean Sullivan who lived on a ranch in the Purgatory Valley. Harlan found a Las Animas County phone book on his shelves in the office and discovered there were a whole bunch of Sullivans who lived in that part of the county. He then called his buddy, Deputy Sheriff Frank Lucero at Trinidad, and asked him if he had any knowledge of Sean Sullivan.

"There are quite a few Sullivans who live in that valley up the Purgatory. Must have been an Irishman in the woodpile somewhere, but now they are all Latino, although some have red hair. Most of them are involved in the cow business, and there are some good ropers in that family," Frank said.

"Does Sean Sullivan have a record?" Harlan asked.

"No, I haven't found any record on him of any kind, but

I'll keep looking."

"Thanks for all your help, Frank. What happened to the Trujillo boys?"

"They are going to stand trial in Raton for the liquor store holdup, but I don't know if the DA there has enough evidence to make it stick. They got a slick lawyer from Santa Fe, so it's doubtful they will spend a day in jail."

"Kinda makes you wonder where they got the money for a slick lawyer?"

"I thought the same thing. Maybe they have resources I don't know about," Frank answered.

"Keep me posted Frank. I'll talk to you later." Harlan signed off.

When Doug and Rita left the dance in Doug's pickup they headed back toward La Veta. He said, "What would you like to do? Do you want to go home?"

"My home has been a tent. In fact, it's already taken down. We just packed up everything and closed down the camp for the winter. This dance thing was a little celebration at the end of this year's encampment," she answered.

"I live in a bunkhouse on a ranch quite a few miles from here," he explained.

"I wouldn't mind bunking up with you for a while," she said coyly, sliding across the pickup seat to snuggle up close to him. "I do need to go by the camp and get my personal gear if you don't mind."

Doug had a grin from ear to ear. The next morning being Sunday, they slept in very late, probably because they had gone to bed so late the night before. There wasn't anyone else living in the bunkhouse at the time so they didn't disturb anyone. BC was a little put out, but he soon got over it when Rita began petting him and stroking his head.

By Monday Doug was back on the job and feeling fine, except for walking a little wobbly-legged. He put in a full day's work near headquarters, taking some food from the cookhouse at noon to Rita. She had spent the day walking around the ranch looking in all the buildings and visiting all the animals who would allow her to pet them. When Doug rode in that evening and put his horse up, he was intercepted on his way to the bunkhouse by Polly.

"Doug, who is that girl that's staying in the bunkhouse?"

"She is a friend who needed a place to stay for a day or two," Doug answered nervously.

"Do you think this looks proper? I have children living here," Polly stated with eyebrows raised.

"How 'bout if I talk to Dub about living at Echo camp. There isn't anyone staying there now, and I'll ask him if it would be okay if I moved up there."

"He's in the office now if you want to talk to him."

"I need to talk to the girl, um, Rita first, if it's okay," he stammered, continuing on toward the bunkhouse.

Echo camp was located about two miles from headquarters and wasn't occupied by a ranch hand because of its close proximity to headquarters. It had a small two-bedroom house inside a white picket fence that enclosed the yard. There was a nice warm barn and several corrals located on a bench up above Echo Canyon.

"Rita," Doug yelled as he came into the bunkhouse. He found her sitting on his bunk, yoga style, reading a *Western Horseman* magazine.

"What is it?" she asked, looking up at Doug.

He pulled off his dirty old black hat and planted a passionate kiss right on her mouth. "I sure missed you today," he said finally.

"I missed you too," she said, kissing him several times.

"How would you feel about moving in with me?" he asked

"I thought I had," she grinned.

"What I mean is I've been thinking all day. There is a little house at another camp not far from here that we could fix up for the two of us, that is," he hesitated, "if you're interested?"

"Doug, what kind of girl do you think I am. If you want to live with me you have to marry me first?" she said teasingly

"Okay, I will," Doug stated.

"Doug, I'm only kidding. Let's spend some time together first. If that works out then, we can get married."

"This place may not suit you. It's kinda remote," Doug said.

"Will you be coming home every day? Coming home to *our* home...to *me* every day?" Rita asked with her eyes full of questions.

"Yes, every day."

"Then it's a deal," she said putting her arms around his sweaty, stinky body and giving him a big hug.

"Let's go over to the boss' house and make sure it's okay."

"You don't know yet?"

"I wanted to talk to you first. Come on. I want you to meet them."

"I need to clean up first, and you need a shower, too," Rita said.

"Maybe we could take a shower together?" Doug suggested.

"If we do that we won't be going anywhere today," Rita said laughing.

After they showered and changed clothes, they walked over to Polly and Dub's house. When the introductions were made, they sat down at the kitchen table. Dub got some beers out of the refrigerator and they had a good discussion. All the details were ironed out and the deal was made.

"I've got one question. What about next summer," Dub asked. "You and John are my main men for tending the cattle in the summer?"

Doug looked dumbfounded, "I don't know. I promised Rita I'd be home every day."

"Not to worry," Rita piped up. "I'd love to go to cow camp with you. I could help you out, and I can ride as good as anyone," she said looking at Doug.

"Granger cow camp ain't much," he said.

"If we are still together by then, it will be fine," Rita said looking deeply into Doug's eyes.

"What do you see in him?" Polly asked Rita.

"He's honest. What he tells you is the truth. Do you know how many truly honest men there are in the world? Most of them would climb a tree to lie to a woman when they could stay on the ground and tell the truth and it would do 'em more good. Besides he has a lot of little boy still in him."

Dub, Polly, and Doug all had big grins on their faces.

"I'm worried about John, though," Doug said.

"If he is not ready to come back, I'm sure Julie and Fro will go back to Sweetwater. If not, then I'll put a young single cowboy at Granger and you guys can go to Sweetwater. Anyway we'll figure it out."

On that same Monday morning Harlan went into the Busy Bee Café for a cup of coffee. There sitting in his favorite booth was Jim Rice, wearing his decorative boots and eating his breakfast. He looked up at Harlan and pointed his fork at the empty seat in the booth, saying, "Have a seat. We need to talk."

"How's it going, Jim?" Harlan asked.

"I'm fine," he said, sounding a bit peeved. "I hear you're asking a lot of questions about me."

"A man is dead. He wasn't killed by a bear. He was murdered, and you're having an affair with that man's wife, so you're damn right I'm asking questions. I'm a lawman and, like you, I take my job seriously," Harlan answered firmly.

Jim stopped chewing and looked intently into Harlan's eyes. "So you come to arrest me or what?"

"No, I don't think you did it, but I want you to tell me

everything you know about Lackey, his wife, or anything else you know about this case. And remember, I know a lot more than you're giving me credit for."

Rice smiled, showing beautiful white teeth. "Okay, you're right. I saw Lackey's wife a few times. We met in a beer joint in Walsenburg and she came on purty strong. Well, that's how it started. I saw her a few times after that, but not in the last few months. She has way too much baggage for me. To her it's more about striking out at her husband than enjoying some sex."

"You were at her house the day I went there for the notification," Harlan stated.

"How did you know that?" Rice said surprised. "I hid my pickup."

"Those," Harlan said, pointing at Rice's boots.

"Well, I'll be damned. You are purty sharp, deputy."

"At any time did Mrs. Lackey suggest that she wanted her husband gone or done away with?"

"No, she was always cussing him to his back because she thought he was messing around with other women. When she started getting possessive with me, I booked."

"Do you know anything about Jim Lackey? Was he having affairs or do you know of anyone who wanted him dead?"

"The only thing I know is his wife thought he was seeing a woman in Trinidad. This was because of something he told her during a big fight. Just convinces me more than ever not to ever get married," Rice added.

"You need to be careful, Jim. Someone's going to walk in on you someday and there may be hell to pay," Harlan warned.

"Is this the deputy in you, or are you worried about my health?"

"I'm here to protect and serve, but I may not be able to watch your back when you're in Alamosa," Harlan smiled, getting up to leave.

Jim Rice watched with a perplexed look on his face as Harlan left the café. An old duffer who had been at the counter drinking coffee and watching the exchange between deputy and brand inspector came over to Jim's booth.

"Why is he asking so many questions? Are you in trouble?" he asked curiously.

"None of your damned business. But I'll tell you one thing, that is one smart Mexican there. I just gained a whole lot of respect for him.

The next day after Doug finished with his ranch work, he and Rita went over to Echo camp in Doug's pickup. When they arrived BC had to go around and sniff every fence post and weed on the place and leave his own territorial marker. Doug went to unlock the front door to the house, but he discovered it was already unlocked. They went in and Rita was going through all the rooms when she called out from the bedroom.

"Someone's been sleeping in my bed!"

When Doug went into the bedroom it was obvious that someone had been using the bed. There weren't any sheets but a couple of blankets were spread on the mattress.

"Looks like someone has been having some fun here," Doug said. "I'm going outside to see if I can find any tracks."

Looking around outside he found tire tracks in the lane that led down to the county road about a half mile to the east. Walking out toward the corral he found horse tracks—a small horse about the size of a pony. These led to and from the corral, and there were more tracks inside the corral.

"So this is where she goes to when she takes her evening rides. I'll bet the vehicle that made those tracks in the lane is a red pickup driven by a red-headed cowboy," he said to himself.

He went into the house to report to Rita what he had found. They decided to go to town and get the household supplies and groceries they would need to set up housekeeping. When they got to the gate at the county road they discovered that a new padlock was installed in the chain securing the gate to the gatepost. Whoever installed this padlock had cut a link out of the chain and attached his own lock in addition to the ranch's padlock. Not having one of the ranch's locks in his personal pickup, Doug made a mental note to bring one from headquarters in order to lock out whoever the intruder was.

Harlan was on traffic patrol one day when he received a call on the radio from Frank Lucero.

"Hey, Harlan. *Que pasa?*" Frank asked.

"It's going good—how about you?"

"I've gotten some more information about Sean Sullivan. He went to college at Lamar State, and he graduated in 1952 with a degree in general studies. He doesn't have a record and has never been in trouble as far as I am able to determine."

"Thanks, Frank. That's not much to go on, but it gives me another lead. Anything new concerning the Trujillo brothers?"

"No, they are out on bail. Their trial don't come up for a couple more months. I have to go, but I'll keep you informed."

"Thanks again, Frank. We'll be talking."

When he was back in his office Harlan called the Admissions Department at Lamar College. Asking about Sean Sullivan, he received the same info that Frank had given him. He asked whether they could send a yearbook for 1952, but they informed him he could only come in person to look at it. He then called the sheriff's office at Lamar and asked if they could go to the college and look at the yearbook. When they agreed, Harlan made copies of Sean and Angela's driver's license photos and mailed them to the deputy in Lamar.

Doug and Rita had been busy. They got the Echo camp house all cleaned up, and they repainted some rooms. They also moved some furniture from headquarters and were getting settled in. The kitchen required the most attention as it looked like a cowboy had lived there. In Rita's words, it was "plenty grungy." She scraped and scrubbed until it was shiny and finally passed inspection.

Doug still had to do his work every day, riding to the winter pasture to feed the cows hay and cottonseed cake when there was snow on the ground. He tried to devote time to riding through the cows every day, if possible, to make sure they were all okay. Dub helped out in this job because, even though he had a lot of managerial duties to keep up with, he liked to put in as much time as possible in the saddle. He was always training a young horse in the art of being a good cow horse, so he combined that job with checking cows. Fro had his area to keep up with and was busy every day with the same tasks.

One evening as Doug was riding Pingo and approaching Echo camp, BC noticed something off to the right. When Doug looked in that direction he saw a paint horse and rider apparently heading to the same place he was. As the rider neared the camp she pulled up and was looking at the house and the yard. Doug's pickup was parked in the yard and the house looked like it was lived in. Doug's other horses were also in the corral. As Doug neared, the rider saw him and wheeled the horse off at a fast trot. Doug knew it was Angela and he expected to see a red pickup pull up to the gate at the county road any minute. "Well, now they know we are here," he mused to BC, who took this info with a wag of his tail.

Harlan was in his office a few days later when he received a call from the sheriff's office at Lamar, Colorado.

"We have done as you requested and took the pictures you sent to the college. We compared them to the graduation photos in the 1952 yearbook. Sean Sullivan is in there all right, but the girl you called Angela Ransom is under a different name. In the yearbook a picture of the same girl is listed as Anne Cimino. We made a copy of her admission records and are mailing them to you along with your photos."

"Thank you very much. This is very helpful to our investigation. If I can ever help you, please let me know. Thanks again," Harlan replied.

He then called his boss and informed him of this new

information. Harlan was told that the bag of trash sent to the state crime lab provided fingerprints only. Unfortunately, the prints were not in the system and could not be identified. He asked them to begin researching a woman named Anne Cimino.

The method of feeding cattle when there was snow on the ground was for a vehicle to drag a couple of old tractor tires through the snow on the feed grounds until it was cleared enough to scatter hay and cottonseed cake. If the snow stayed on the ground, this was done every day. This required a tractor, a large truck to haul hay, and a pickup with a "cake" box on the back to distribute the cake.

One year soon after Doug started working at the ranch, the bean counters decided this process was too expensive. What with all the fuel costs, the mileage, plus wear and tear on the equipment and vehicles, they decided to do all the winter feeding with teams and wagons. At that time the ranch had a large horse herd with a few teams of work horses and mules left over from when everything was done that way. This stock was kept in an area called the Horse Pasture, where they had been living the good life with no responsibilities at all. Suddenly all the stock in this pasture was rounded up, the work horse teams cut out, and a dramatic change took place in their lives.

Doug and John Latham, who was working full time for

the ranch back then, were assigned a team of big red mules who were both from a Percheron mare and a mammoth jack. They were brothers only one year apart in age, and they were huge in size—about fourteen hands at the shoulder and weighing about thirteen hundred pounds each. Neither one ever had so much as a halter on him. When driven into a corral they acted like wild animals.

Doug and John managed to get them into a round pen used for breaking horses. For several days the mules were watered and fed there. They were roped and snubbed to a large post in the middle of the pen, individually of course, and were introduced to the bridle. The workhorse bridle is quite different from a riding bridle, having blinders that prevent the horse or mule from looking backward. An equine has the ability to see backward as well as forward, and he can aim a kick very accurately by glancing back. The blinders are one way to prevent this from happening.

After the bridles were installed the mules were driven around the pen to teach them how to turn in response to the reins. Of course, being mules, they were very stubborn about this, but they eventually learned that the two hard-headed cowboys were more stubborn than they were. Next it was back to the snubbing post where the harness was placed on their backs. There were the usual protests with much bucking, squealing, and hee-hawing, but as they did with the bridles they finally accepted the harness. There were more sessions of trotting around the pen, getting used to the harness with all its rattling and clattering.

Finally after a few days it was time to hook them up to a wagon, and several rigs were dragged out of a barn where they had been in storage for years. Some repair work was needed, but soon they were declared serviceable. Doug and John decided to pull the wagon over to the loading chute where eighteen-wheelers loaded cattle. The chutes were held up by two large steel pipes buried in concrete. This design prevented overzealous truck drivers from damaging the loading chutes when they backed up their big rigs to be loaded. The eighteen-wheeler's trailer might get damaged, but the chute wouldn't budge. Doug and John laid the tongue of the wagon up on the top chute. They planned to bring the mules out and tie them with very strong halter ropes, one to each post. This worked fine with only a few glitches the first time they tried it. They placed their Levi jackets over the mule's heads as a precaution to make sure they couldn't look back.

The most dangerous part of the whole operation was hooking up the trace chains (part of the harness) to the wagon's singletree. One well-placed kick could maim or kill. The mules could not see backward, but they could sense that someone was behind them, so they kicked blindly several times. The cowboys had to watch for the bunching of muscles in the haunches and quickly duck out of the way. Finally everything was hooked up. John got up on the seat, filled his hands with reins, and put his foot on the brake. Doug slipped up beside the head of the mule on the right, taking off the jacket and untying the halter rope. He very carefully tied the halter rope to the harness and then went around and did the same thing to the other mule.

As soon as he got the halter rope tied up to that mule's harness and was fixin' to get up on the wagon seat with John, all hell broke loose. The mules realized they were no longer tied and started running as fast as they could go, dragging the wagon after them. John was stomping on the brakes and pulling on the reins and cussing as loudly as he could. Doug was running along behind, yelling for them to wait for him. The mules made a few circles around the ranch yard and then headed down the road. There was a five strand barbed wire gate about a quarter mile down this road, and John figured they would stop there. Not a chance! They hit that gate at full speed, taking out the gate and about two hundred yards of fence, after the gate got tangled up in the wagon.

Doug witnessed all of this and the last thing he saw was the wagon bouncing into the air in a big cloud of dust, and John flapping around, sometimes coming down on the seat and sometimes not. Doug decided to go back and get a Dodge Power Wagon to follow the catastrophe by pickup. About two miles down the road he found John, who looked like he had been through a war, sitting on the ground beside the road. The mules and wagon were down in a ditch, the wagon turned over and thoroughly wrecked.

The mules were played out so Doug got them unhitched and tied to the back of the pickup. After several trips they finally were able to get everything back to camp. A couple of days later, after getting all the repairs made that they could, they tried the whole process over again. These cowboys may have been short on brainpower but they were long on determination.

This time they parked a pickup hooked to a horse trailer across the road in front of the repaired gate, thinking the mules surely wouldn't try to run over that. They got the mules all harnessed and hooked up with only a few close calls. Doug got his hat kicked off, but the hoof only grazed his hard head. Doug untied the halter ropes and lifted the coats from the mules heads, then sprinted for the wagon. John had a firm grip on the reins and was practically standing on the brake when the mules made their break. Doug managed to grab the tailgate and swing himself aboard the wagon, only wishing a minute later that he was back on solid ground.

John kept a tight pull on the rein of the right-hand mule, trying to get them to run in a circle until they played out. Round and round they went in the yard. They stirred up so much dust that it looked like a tornado was hitting the ranch. Doug was rolling and tossing in the back of the wagon like a sack of potatoes. After several trips around the yard the mules began to tire and finally settled down to a trot. This allowed Doug to join John on the wagon seat.

"I believe these sombitches are gonna be all right," John declared with a big grin.

They worked the team for another hour or so until they had them turning and steering just like they were supposed to.

"Tomorrow we'll load the wagon before we hook up and head for the feed ground," John said optimistically.

The next day instead of feeding first by truck and coming back to camp for the mule training session, they loaded the wagon with hay and cake and parked it in front of the loading chutes. This time they opened the gate that was down the road. They took the usual precautions in getting hooked up, and then took off down the road at a fast trot. The mules began to tire after a mile or so and slowed down to a nice even ground-covering trot. They soon traveled the three miles or so to the feed ground.

When the cattle saw the wagonload of feed heading their way they started gathering and coming toward the wagon. This made the mules nervous and they picked up the speed a bit. John was trying to get them to slow down but to no avail. Doug was doing his best to throw out hay and shovel cake while the wagon was bouncing, but it was hard enough just to hang on. Finally the job was done and the cowboys were congratulating each other on their way home.

Things went fairly well for several feedings when John declared one day that instead of pulling the wagon by pickup to the cake bin to fill it, they would hook up the mules and let them get used to the bin and the filling process. The cake bin is a huge steel container on steel beam stilts, and it holds about twenty tons of cottonseed cake. The cake is made from cottonseed residue, molasses, and other good stuff that cattle love. It's a good source of protein and an excellent supplement to winter feed. Pickups with cake feeders or wagons can be pulled under the cake bin and be filled from a chute.

All went fairly well, even though the mules were wary of the huge bin towering over them. They went under and stopped just right so that the chute was directly over the wagon. Doug got ahold of the lever that allowed the cake to come out and asked,

"Are you ready?"

"I'm as ready as I'm gonna be," answered John, standing on the brake and holding the reins tight.

The cake had to drop about six or seven feet to the wagon bed, so when it hit the wagon it made a purty good racket. This was more than the mules could stand and they took off like a shot, veering to the right as they did. This caused the back wheel of the wagon to catch one of the upright beams, which ripped the wheel completely off the wagon. When the wheel came off Doug went flying and was picking himself up spitting dirt when John finally got the mules stopped. Now they had two wrecked wagons with only one left.

About a week later they were on their way to a feed ground that was nearly six miles from camp when they had another big wreck. The mules had finally gotten used to the noises of filling the wagon and were generally doing purty good in their new job. They would still kick a bit if they thought it would be productive, but all in all they had calmed down a lot.

They were walking along about half asleep, the cowboys riding in the wagon about half asleep, when a jackrabbit burst out of the weeds beside the road and nearly went under the mule on the left. This spooked him and he took off running, which spooked his brother, and the race was on. John was yelling and cussing and stomping on the brake. Doug was trying to hold on and keep his hat from flying. Hay and cake was being scattered all over the road, but there weren't any cows there to eat it.

In a few hundred yards the road turned sharply to the right, as there was a deep arroyo straight ahead. The mules turned at the last second but the wagon went over the edge, pulling the mules along with it. The cowboys jumped just at the last second and suffered only bumps, bruises, and a few scrapes. When they got up and walked to the arroyo to look in, one mule was down on his side tangled in the harness and looking injured. The other was also tangled but standing. The wagon tongue had snapped in two and their last wagon was a total wreck.

"Dag nab it!" yelled John, who just a minute before had picked up his hat and dusted it off, but now threw it back on the ground and stomped on it.

When they had first started this feeding project they always tied a saddle horse on the back of the wagon just in case they had a wreck some distance from camp. On this particular day they were feeling so confident that they hadn't brought the horse.

Doug said very sorrowfully and rhetorically, "Do you know how far we are from camp?"

After thinking about this for a moment John said, "You go get a truck while I get these mules untangled."

A cowboy hates to walk. There is an old story about a cowboy who rides up to a gate, gets off to open it, gets back on, rides his horse through, then gets back off to close the gate. A lot of this perambulatory hatred is because of their footwear. Cowboy boots are the most uncomfortable things to walk in. Doug reluctantly took off walking back to camp, arriving almost two hours later. He fired up one of the old pickups and went to retrieve John. Upon arriving he saw one of the mules out of the arroyo and tied to a tree. The other was still laying down in the bottom. The mule had broken a leg so John used his ever-present pistol to put him out of his misery. John had to cut the harness off the surviving mule, so there was a dead mule, a totally wrecked wagon, and a pile of useless harness lying in the bottom of the arroyo.

"You know the name of this arroyo?" asked John.

"No, what's its name?"

"Mule Wreck Arroyo," answered John disgustedly.

Harlan had been gathering information from several sources and he came to the conclusion that Angela Ransom had only existed since her arrival in the La Veta area. The woman by the name of Anne Cimino had been born in Liberal, Kansas, and after graduating from high school went to Lamar State College. After graduating from there, however, Anne Cimino ceased to exist.

Why would a young person want to change her identity? The only thing Harlan could come up with was that she was trying to hide something. But what, and was this tied to Lackey's murder? He discussed it with his boss, the sheriff, and with Celeste, and they both agreed with him. He decided to approach it from a different angle and do a background check on the murder victim. Maybe there was some connection between these two people or between Sullivan and Lackey.

Rita and Doug had the little Echo camp house all fixed up into a cozy little love nest, thanks mostly to Rita's hard work and ability to turn a sow's ear into a silk purse.

Doug had been used to living in cow camps or bunkhouses for years and was comfortable with much simpler things—not that he didn't appreciate the feminine touch, because he did. Overall he was a much more contented cowboy now.

The winter was cold with lots of snow, so ice in the tanks and tubs had to be chopped every morning for the stock to get water. Whenever the ground was covered with snow the cattle had to be fed, thankfully not with teams and wagons anymore. The bean counters had decided it was cheaper to feed with tractors and trucks after all the calamities of feeding with wagons. Doug really enjoyed returning to a warm and loving home after a long, hard day in the cold.

One Saturday Rita and Doug went to town to buy groceries and supplies. They had driven one of the ranch's one ton Power Wagon flatbed trucks loaded with hay. This was at the suggestion of Dub who wanted the hay delivered to John Latham's place. He knew John wasn't able to rustle up any hay so he asked Doug to deliver it. When Rita and Doug finished their shopping, they went to the Latham's and unloaded the hay in the barn with Albert's help. Then they went into the house to visit with John and Sonja.

"How ya doin' John?" Doug asked as they came in.

John was up and had answered the door. He was using a cane and had a removable brace on his left leg.

"I'm doing much better. Almost ready to run a hundred yard dash," he answered with a grin. "Thanks for the hay. That'll really help out."

"Thank Dub. He gave us the order to bring it to you."

"He sure has been a real pard' through all this. He's a good man and a good boss."

"So I see you're walking purty good. What does the doc

say?"

"They just tell me to keep doing physical therapy, to keep trying to bend the knee and walk as much as I can stand it," John answered, settling into his easy chair and waving Doug to the sofa. Rita and Sonja were visiting in the kitchen.

"Do you think you'll be able to go back to work someday?" Doug asked.

"I sure hope so. I'm getting fat and lazy lying around here. I've been working in my shop out there in the garage, making bits, spurs, bridles, and other tack. If you need anything let me know," John answered.

"I could use another bosal. I'm working a couple of colts this winter in my spare time."

"I've got a whole spool of good stout cord. I'll plait one for you."

"How much?"

"How 'bout fifteen bucks?"

"Done."

"So how's the winter feeding going? You feeding with wagons this year?" John chuckled.

"No, thank God. I hope we never have to do that again. But if we do, we need a nice docile team like Fro had," Doug said laughing. "It's going well, the cattle look good, the cows should be dropping calves in about a month, so we'll have to keep a close watch on them when that starts."

"Make sure they're close to some timber so they can get out of the wind when they start calving," John suggested.

"We're moving the feed grounds closer to timber every day, but we need you out there to help us when we start pulling calves."

"I wished I could be there. You don't know how much I wish for that."

"I don't know, maybe you're lucky. That is a cold, wet, miserable job and usually in the middle of the night," Doug answered.

"Don't kid me—you love it—you know you do," John said.

"You don't have to be crazy to do this job—but it sure helps," Doug answered.

Harlan had submitted the background check on Jim Lackey, and he was sitting at his desk when the envelope arrived with the results. One interesting connection was that Lackey had been born in Kansas and had lived and worked in Liberal for a period of time in the early fifties. He thought this was too much of a coincidence, so he asked the county sheriff's office in Liberal for their assistance. The next day Harlan received a phone call from Sheriff Williams of Seward County, Kansas.

"I understand you are looking for background information about a Jim Lackey."

"Yes, sir. I'm working a murder investigation in Huerfano County, Colorado. Jim Lackey was killed in our area last June. Some of the latest leads I'm following have turned up a connection in Liberal, Kansas. Can you tell me anything about Lackey's past or what he did while living in Kansas?"

"It peaked my interest when I found out he had been killed, which is why I called you right back. In the early fifties Lackey was working at a bank in Liberal. He was a young assistant teller, and he did whatever they needed him to do, including sweeping out the place. In January of 1951 that bank was robbed. A significant amount of cash was taken and the robbers got away. It's still in our cold case file."

"Did you suspect Lackey of being involved at the time?" Harlan asked.

"I suspected a lot of things at the time, but could not come up with anything conclusive," Sheriff Williams answered.

"What kind of person was Lackey? Did his boss or fellow employees say anything about him?"

"According to everyone I questioned, Lackey thought pretty highly of himself. He seemed to be quite a ladies' man and put the move on some of the women who worked at the bank. He was not that good looking but that didn't deter him."

"Were any of the robbers identified?"

"No, they both wore dark clothing, black ski masks, and gloves. But a couple of eye-witnesses were purty sure one of the robbers was a woman. They escaped in a nondescript gray sedan that was found the next day in an out-of-the way place in the Oklahoma panhandle. The vehicle had been completely burned out. In fact it was several days before we decided it was the getaway car."

"Did you ever suspect that Lackey might have been involved? That it might have been an inside job?"

"Not at the time. He was lying face down like everyone else in the bank during the robbery."

"You suggested that you had some suspicions. What made you think afterward that he might have been involved?"

"Only that about eight months later he quit and moved away. I had been monitoring his bank account along with others but never found anything out of the ordinary or any excessive spending, so I had to abandon that line of inquiry."

"One other name that has come up in my investigation of the Lackey murder is a woman by the name of Anne Cimino. Does that name mean anything to you?" Harlan asked.

"Hmm, there was a car dealer here for a while by the name of Cimino. How old would this person be?"

"Late twenties or early thirties."

"Possibly a daughter, but I'll have to look into that," the sheriff answered.

"I think she graduated from Liberal High School in the late forties."

"I'll check that out and call you back. If you find anything that will help me close my cold case, please let me know."

"Yes sir, I surely will. I'm looking forward to hearing from you again," Harlan said signing off.

Doug and John had moved into the kitchen to join the ladies who had some delicious pie and coffee ready.

"Rita, didn't you say you worked for a while at Bear Mountain Scout Ranch in Cimarron, New Mexico?" John asked.

"Yes, I worked there for three years. Why?" Rita replied.

"Last spring we had a cowboy here helping with the branding who was from that ranch. His name was Steve Sheldon."

"Yes, I know Steve very well. He is a good friend and an old drinking buddy. There is a wonderful historical center at Bear Mountain, and Steve is the museum curator," Rita answered. "I didn't know he was up here last spring."

"Yeah, he was here for about a week at the invitation of Dub. He lived in the bunkhouse and he and I had some interesting discussions. Steve is definitely a cowboy historian and a real authority concerning Will James."

"He's been a paraplegic since he had polio as a child, but once he is in the saddle you could never guess it," Doug added.

John piped in, "He can do some amazing things with a rope and, once in the saddle, he is one of the best cowhands I've ever had the pleasure of knowing in my life."

"That dun horse he was riding is no slouch either," Doug remarked with a touch of envy in his voice.

"Yeah, that is one good piece of horseflesh. That cowboy and that horse sorta complement each other," John said. "I wonder if he's coming back this year?"

"We'll have to ask Dub. I sure hope you are there," Doug stated, looking over at John.

"Me too," John said.

"Me too," Sonja and Rita said in unison.

In the meantime, Harlan was trying to piece all his evidence together and see what his next steps should be. The fact that Angela or Anne used to live in the same small town as the victim was too much of a coincidence, especially since Doug found her horse's track near the murder scene. Also the girl had changed her identity, or tried to. He decided to consult his boss to see if he had enough evidence to bring her in for questioning.

The sheriff decided to discuss it with the District Attorney to get his opinion. They both agreed they didn't have enough proof to bring her in for questioning, but that Harlan could go back to her workplace and talk to her informally. They decided that an official interrogation might cause her to run.

Harlan went to the library and returned the Louis L'Amour book he had checked out previously. He was browsing through some other titles when Angela approached him.

"Well, I see you're back, and did you like that book?" she asked.

"Yes, I read all these when I was a kid, but I do enjoy reading them again," he answered. "So how you doing?" he asked casually.

"Fine. How are Celeste and your children?"

"They are all good—looking forward to Christmas."

"That's good," she answered beginning to move off.

"I was wondering if you could help me. I have been investigating the suspicious death of someone I think you might know. Do you have time to answer a couple of questions?" he asked.

Harlan caught the sudden look of panic in her eyes that she tried to quickly mask.

"What makes you think I can help you?" she said defensively.

Harlan decided to use his "I know more about this than you think I know" tactic.

"I have been investigating this case for about six months and have found a lot of information. I think it's time to start being honest with me, don't you?"

"Am I under arrest?" she asked defiantly.

"No, Angela, please... I just need to ask you some questions."

"I won't talk to you anymore unless my lawyer is present," she stated emphatically.

"Lawyer! You are certainly escalating this," he said, getting out his hand cuffs.

"What!" A look of horror came across her face.

"Angela Ransom, I'm arresting you on suspicion of withholding evidence," Harlan said. He explained her rights and clicked the hand cuffs on her wrists.

Doug and Rita had left the Latham's and were driving toward Echo camp.

"What are those stains on your hat?" Rita asked. "Looks like poop."

"Some of them might be," he said, "maybe several different kinds."

"What do you mean?"

"Well, last summer my horse threw me and I landed head first in a big ol' fresh cow pie...and before that a bear pooped on me."

"How did that happen?" Rita asked laughing.

"I rode up on a young black bear one day last summer. BC and I took out after him and he ran up a tree. I was at the base of the tree making a fuss over BC for doing such a good job when the bear pooped on me. It hit on top of my hat and then slid off onto my shoulder. The bear had evidently been eating something dead because it sure did stink. I shook my fist at the bear, but all he did was grin back at me. When I went to mount my horse the bear came down and took off running again.

I was still feeling a bit put out, so I took down my rope and spurred off after him. I was riding ol' Slim, who is real quick, and soon got a loop around the bear's head and over one shoulder. Slim turned to the left like he would if it were a steer, and the bear went rolling when he hit the end of that rope. I guess I had visions of tying him up like a calf because I dismounted and was following my rope down to the bear, with my piggin' string in hand, when he finally got to his feet. He figured I was responsible for all his troubles and came charging at me. I was pushing on that rope for all I was worth, to no avail. You can pull on a rope with some effect, but pushing on one doesn't do anything," Doug said hesitating.

"Well, don't stop there! What happened?" Rita asked excitedly.

"BC saved my bacon. He barreled into that bear and they both went rolling. When the dust cleared the bear was running off and BC came back to me with tongue lolled out and looking very proud of himself. One glance at him told me what he was thinking: "There, I saved your ass again."

Harlan got Angela loaded in his unit and hauled her to the courthouse in Walsenburg where he deposited her in an interrogation room. Soon he was joined by Sheriff Ed Sisneros and the DA, Roy Stevens. After a briefing, they all went into the interrogation room together.

"I don't understand why you dragged me here," Angela

protested as Harlan removed her hand cuffs.

"Has anyone read you your rights?" the DA asked.

"Rights, why would you need to read me my rights?"

"Did Deputy Martinez read you your rights before you were brought here?"

"Yes, he did, but I don't understand why it was necessary to drag me to jail," she asked scornfully.

"I tried to ask you some simple questions, Angela, and you refused to respond. Now it's time to tell the truth," Harlan stated emphatically.

The DA began, "Angela... or should we call you Anne. We know when you were born, where you went to school, and where you went to college. We know a lot about you when you went by the name of Anne Cimino. Why did you change your name in 1952 to Angela Ransom?"

A look of fear and bewilderment appeared on the face of the girl before she stated, "There is no law against changing your name."

"Not if it's done legally, in court, which yours was not," the DA responded.

"Do you know this man?" the DA asked, placing a photo of Jim Lackey in front of Angela.

She barely glanced at it, "I want a lawyer, and I'm not saying another word until my lawyer is present." She said looking down at her lap.

After Angela made a couple of phone calls, they placed her in a cell.

"You can't put me in jail. I've done nothing wrong," she protested.

"We can hold you for twenty-four hours. If in the meantime we find more evidence, we can amend our arrest order. This could have been avoided if you would just tell the truth."

"The DA is going to look at this failure to cooperate in a very bad light. I'm afraid for you Angela. Things are not looking good right now," Harlan advised her.

"I have to talk to my lawyer first," she said crying.

Angela would spend a cold, lonesome night in the county jail. Harlan went home to his wife but came back to the courthouse early the next morning. There he found Sully, the cowboy he had previously seen with Angela, sitting on a bench in a hallway of the courthouse. When Sully saw Harlan he rose and came toward him.

"They won't let me see Angela. What have you charged her with, and what is going on?" Sully asked.

"Let's go in here and talk," Harlan suggested, leading Sully into an interrogation room.

"Can I get you a coffee or anything," Harlan asked. "I know I need some."

"Yeah, coffee would be good," Sully answered.

When Harlan brought two steaming cups of coffee they sat down at the table.

"All of this can be cleared up very easily with a few straight answers," Harlan said.

In a minute they were joined by the sheriff and the DA whom Harlan called when he went to get the coffee.

"We tried to find out from Angela why she changed her name and if she had any knowledge of Jim Lackey. She refused to answer and insisted on a lawyer. We know the answer to some of these questions, but we'd like an explanation from her," Harlan explained to Sully.

"I don't know what you think I can add," Sully said.

"Look, we know you and Angela are an item. We know you've had a long-term relationship with her, that you and she had a courtship starting in college or maybe before. We know that Angela had a connection to Jim Lackey. Those are just a few of the things we know. We think you know why she changed her name, and we just want you to tell us why," the DA stated.

"I need to talk to Angela first before I answer any of your questions," Sully responded.

"You seem like a smart person, Sean. You should realize that things will be better for you and everyone concerned if you tell the truth. Right now this interview is informal. Please be advised that we will find out the truth, and it will go much better for you if you tell us all you know," the sheriff advised.

"Angela is innocent. She didn't have anything to do with anything."

"How are we supposed to know that if no one will tell us what's been going on?" the DA said impatiently.

"She didn't have anything to do with what?" Harlan asked.

"I can't tell you anything more. I need to see Angela," Sean insisted.

They left Sean or "Sully" in the interview room by himself and walked down the hall to the sheriff's office. "Do we charge him?" asked the sheriff.

"No, not yet," said the DA. "I'm issuing a search warrant for his house, outbuildings and vehicles, and I'll send it for immediate execution to the sheriff's office in Trinidad. If they can search his place before he gets back home, maybe they can find a black powder rifle. Don't let him or Angela know about this until the search is completed. Also, we'd better do a search of her vehicle and house. I want you to do that, Deputy Martinez."

"How about the Library in La Veta where she works?" asked Harlan?

"Good idea. Also his pickup—do we know where it is?"

"It's out there in the parking lot. I saw it on my way in," Harlan said.

"Get it searched also," the DA said looking at the sheriff. "These cowboys like to carry their guns on a rack in their trucks. While all of this is going on, the sheriff and I will interview Angela with her lawyer present, and maybe we will invite Sean to an interview, too."

When Doug looked out the window in the morning he noticed that a big snow had come during the night. It was very early, but Doug knew the cows needed to be fed and some mama's that were close to calving needed to be checked, so he started to put on his long johns and jeans. Over this he would wear Carhartt coveralls to keep out the wind, and overshoes to protect his feet from the numbing cold. Rita, who was still under a pile of quilts, began to stir.

"Doug," she mumbled.

"Yes darlin," he said lifting a corner of the quilt so he could see her pretty face.

"We need to talk," she said.

"What now—you're barely awake."

"I've been dreaming and thinking, and I'm pretty sure I'm pregnant," she stated.

"Yahoo! Are you sure?" Doug said excitedly jumping up and down.

"Wow, you really are excited about this. I didn't know how you were going to take it," she said sitting up and taking in his antics.

"This is fantastic news! When do you think the baby will be born?" he asked.

"Maybe August or September, if I'm pregnant and calculated right."

"This is the best news ever. We are going to make fantastic parents—I just know it."

"There is just one little thing that we need to discuss. We need to get married first." She looked up at him expectantly.

"There is no problem there. We can do that as soon as possible, if you'll have me."

"What time is it?" she asked, looking at the dark window.

"It's a little after five. A big snow came during the night and I need to go feed."

"I'll fix you some breakfast first. You'll need to stay warm," she said getting up and getting dressed.

"Why don't you stay in bed. You need to take care of yourself now," he said with a concerned look on his face.

"I'm pregnant, not an invalid. Pioneer women stopped for a short while to have a kid, and then they went on with their chores. I'm going with you today so that we can discuss all the plans we need to make."

When they arrived at headquarters to fill the cake box on the back of the truck, they noticed Harlan's official vehicle coming up the road, so they went to meet him. The vehicles pulled up beside each other, driver's door to driver's door.

"Hey cowboy, how's it going?" Harlan asked.

"It's going wonderful—were pregnant!" Doug answered.

"That's great news. You guys are quick."

"I think its wonderful news. Yeah, I'm not getting any younger so we have to be quick."

"We're going to get married soon and we want you and Celeste to stand with us," Rita said beaming.

"We would be proud to. When is that going to happen?" Harlan asked.

"Soon—we have to make the arrangements and we'll let you know. When is a good time for you guys?" Rita asked.

"Weekends are best for both of us. I'm getting real busy with this Lackey case now, and Celeste teaches every weekday."

"How is that case going?" Doug asked. "I haven't heard anything about it in a while."

"That's what I'm doing here today. I have a warrant to search Angela's place," Harlan stated.

"We have to go feed cows, but I have a suggestion. You might want to search that little barn behind her house. When I went there to look at her horse's hoofs to see if they made the tracks I saw in the mountains, I remembered something sounding like metal on metal when the horse set the hoof back down. At the time I thought it was a loose shoe, but the shoe didn't appear to be loose. There might be something buried under the floor of that barn," Doug said.

"Thanks, I'll check it out. Let us know about the wedding."

"We will. Tell Celeste and the kids hello from us."

When Harlan executed the search warrant he took Doug's advice and started at the barn. He had borrowed a spade from the ranch and began digging in the dirt floor of the stall where Angela's horse stayed most of the time. On the third thrust into the ground the shovel hit something hard that sounded like metal. He went to the house and called out another deputy who was assisting with the search. The deputy had the camera, so they could capture photographic evidence of him digging up a metal box. They carried the box to the house in order to have other witnesses present when they opened it.

The box was a little larger than a shoe box and looked like it might have been an old military ammo box. It smelled of horse poop and urine, and looked like it had been buried for a long time. It was watertight and rusted shut. After some effort they finally got it open. Inside was a lot of money, mostly wrapped in the original bank wrappers with the name *Citizens State Bank—Liberal Kansas* on the wrapper bands.

Having found nothing else, the deputies put the box in an evidence bag, placed it in Harlan's unit, and headed back to the courthouse in Walsenburg. Harlan radioed the sheriff's office and explained what they had found. The sheriff and the DA resumed their questioning of Angela.

"Now that you have your lawyer present, are you ready to tell us what it is that you have been trying to hide?" the DA asked Angela.

"I'm not trying to hide anything. I want to go home," she said defiantly.

"I demand that you either charge my client or let her go. You have had her in custody too long already," her lawyer, a Mr. Salazar, demanded.

"Okay, we'll do that. We'll be charging your client with bank robbery in a short while. Deputy Martinez is bringing in the evidence that we recovered from the place you rent at the Circle Cross Ranch," the DA explained.

Angela blanched when she heard this bit of news. She quickly leaned over to whisper something in her lawyer's ear.

"I need to confer with my client," the lawyer said.

When Harlan arrived at the courthouse he met with the sheriff and the DA, showing them the new evidence. The sheriff informed him that the Las Animas County Sheriff's

Department had executed a search warrant on Sean Sullivan's place and found a fifty caliber black powder rifle in a dugout storage building located in a canyon behind his ranch buildings. A Huerfano County deputy was dispatched to Trinidad to pick it up.

"Bring Mr. Sullivan into the room with Ms. Cimino, and bring that box in also," the DA said.

They re-entered the interview room with the sheriff escorting Sean. Harlan carried the metal box which was inside a large evidence bag. When they entered the room Sean and Angela exchanged looks and Angela shook her head imperceptibly from side to side. Sean pulled up a chair and sat down beside Angela, holding her hands in his. Harlan put the box down on the table.

"Do either of you recognize this?" the DA asked.

Neither one responded.

"This was found in the barn behind the house you rent at the Circle Cross Ranch, Miss Cimino. We will be sending it to the crime lab to see if there are any fingerprints on it or its contents. The Las Animas County Sheriff's Department searched your place, Mr. Sullivan, and found a fifty caliber black powder rifle on your property. We will also send it to the crime lab to see if there is any forensic evidence to link it to the weapon used to kill Mr. Jim Lackey last June. Does anyone wish to make a statement?"

"I have been trying to cooperate with you. Why would you search my place?" Sean asked.

"Do you have a lawyer, Mr. Sullivan, or is Mr. Salazar representing you both?" the DA asked.

"I don't know. I didn't know I needed a lawyer. I need to speak with Mr. Salazar and Angela in private," Sean answered.

"Okay, you folks talk it over. What we need here is the truth. Mr. Salazar, I recommend you advise these people to tell the truth. I will be much more lenient in pressing charges if they do so," the DA explained.

"I demand that you let my client and Mr. Sullivan free. You haven't charged them with anything yet, and all you have is circumstantial evidence. You don't have enough for a conviction," Mr. Salazar declared.

"I've convicted on less evidence than this, so we'll see how a jury of Huerfano County folks feels about it," the DA answered. "But if you want charges, I'll file charges for conspiracy to commit murder. Mr. Martinez, read them their rights and book them into the County Jail pending trial," he continued.

"Yes, sir," Harlan said as he read the two their rights and handcuffed them. All this time Angela was crying and clinging to Sean before being handcuffed. Mr. Salazar reassured them that he would do all he could to help them legally.

Rita and Doug were married on New Year's Eve at a beautiful little chapel in La Veta. Celeste and Harlan were bridesmaid and best man. Sonja, John, and their kids attended, plus Polly, Dub, their kids, and all the ranch hands and their families from the Circle Cross. Jennifer, Bobby, and their children plus many other friends and acquaintances from the area were there. The chapel was packed. Afterward a reception was held at the American Legion Hall in La

Veta and a good time was had by all. The newlyweds went to Tucson, Arizona, for their honeymoon to get a few days of warm sun and a break from the cold winter. Fro took over Doug's chores while he was gone.

Shortly after getting back on the job, some of the cows started calving, so there were many sleepless nights while Doug was taking care of the mamas. He would drive one of the old Power Wagon trucks to the calving grounds. This truck was equipped with a gas operated South Wind heater in the cab which made it warm and toasty.

If a newborn was having a little trouble standing or handling the cold temperatures, Doug would put it in the cab of the truck to get warmed up and dried out. In a short while the calf was ready to get back to mama and get a bellyful of warm milk. One of the problems with this procedure was usually after a calf is born it gets its digestive system working properly and it poops. It doesn't really smell bad, but it can sure mess up the seat of a pickup truck.

Many nights Rita went with Doug to help out but usually spent the wee hours of the morning curled up asleep with a baby calf on the seat of the pickup. The mamas were so used to Doug that they didn't mind him tending their babies, with the exception of some young cows who weren't familiar with the routine. Sometimes these mamas would chase him behind a tree or into the pickup. Fro had the biggest problem with irate mothers because he had all the first-calf heifers to contend with. Normally the last week of January and the first two weeks of February was when the majority of the calves were born. There usually was a warming spell during this time, but not always. Mother Nature had a way of fooling even the smartest of humans.

Harlan was summoned to the courthouse one day in early February. When he arrived the sheriff explained that they received the forensic report from the state crime lab. The prints on the metal box found in the barn at Angela's house were partials and inconclusive. Also it was impossible to determine for sure whether the lead embedded in Lackey's spine came from Sean Sullivan's black powder rifle. There was fingerprint evidence on some of the paper bands around the bills inside the metal box that belonged to Lackey. The sheriff pointed out that a good defense lawyer would argue that since Lackey worked at the bank, it would be natural for his fingerprints to be on the paper bands around the money.

The sheriff of Seward County, Kansas, was notified that the money had been recovered, and he responded by driving to Walsenburg. The money found in the box was definitely identified as part of the cash taken in the bank robbery eight years before. In fact it was exactly one third of the total amount taken. Sheriff Williams pointed out that, if Huerfano County failed to bring a case for murder, his jurisdiction wanted to try for a charge of bank robbery.

Both suspects were granted bail and cautioned not to leave the jurisdiction. Sean had retained his own lawyer, a Mr. Frederici from Trinidad. Both lawyers argued that the evidence was only circumstantial and that both suspects should be released on bail, and the judge agreed. Angela and Sean had returned to their own homes and regular jobs.

> "It looks like unless one of them confesses to what happened, we may not be able to convict them," the sheriff said.

> "I thought we had enough evidence," Harlan replied disappointedly. "I guess I need to keep digging."

> "I'm not sure there is anything else you could have done. We may have all the evidence we're going to get," the

sheriff answered.

Rita and Doug had gone to bed early one night, after a particularly hard day of ranch work, when Rita noticed Doug rubbing his left leg. She had been reading and became aware that he seemed to be in a lot of pain.

"Are you all right?" she asked, rolling over towards him.

"It just hurts like hell when it's cold, and I've been on my feet too much," he said.

"Lay down here and let me rub it. I've got healing hands," she said.

"Aaah, that feels good," he said as Rita gently rubbed the scars that ran from his left calf up his thigh to his hip.

"All you've ever said is that this happened in the war. Would you like to tell me more about how it happened?" she asked gently.

"I don't like to talk about it too much, but I guess I can tell you. I was an infantryman in the Army and was sent to Korea. My company was sent to the front lines to help stop the push the North Koreans were making. They had already driven the Allied forces down into South Korea."

"Our company started out with twenty four men and a lieutenant. Six months later we were down to ten men and a sergeant—me. I had been promoted when our company sergeant was killed. We were on the line one night huddling in foxholes to keep out the cold when suddenly some flares went off. As I looked out toward the enemy I saw that one of our scouts who had been doing a recon was trying to make it back to the line. The enemy saw him about the same time as I did and started firing."

"He fell to the ground and started yelling for help. The flares had dimmed, but I could still see purty well. I ran out there, picked him up, and almost made it back to the foxhole when the flares lit up again and the enemy started firing. I felt something hit me and I fell but managed to get up. Just then a mortar shell exploded close to me and literally blew me and the scout down into our trench."

"Thank God for combat medics! They took care of me, got me on a litter, and carried me back to a MASH unit where I was patched up enough to go to a hospital ship. Eventually I made it back to the States and spent a couple of years in and out of VA hospitals. I had several operations and a lot of physical therapy that gave me the use of my leg again. So that's the whole story, and all I got out of it was this ugly scar and a couple of medals."

"Thank God you survived, and thank God the family jewels were not injured," Rita said teasingly.

"It came awful close—look at that!" They both laughed.

"The conclusion I came to from all of this was that I hate war. No one hates war more than someone who has been in the thick of it. Mankind has got to come up with a better plan than this for settling differences. I firmly believe that if the hawks and people who are always getting us into war had to spend some time on the front line or have their children placed in the middle of the fighting, there would be no wars."

"If women, specifically mothers, made the decisions, there would be no wars," Rita stated.

"Wars have never settled anything. Usually after a whole lot of people are killed the negotiators sit down and come up with a peace plan. Why didn't they do that before the war started? There are no winners in war—only survivors. I've noticed that a lot of very rich people get a whole lot richer during a war. It's almost like they planned it that way," Doug avowed.

"Kids, young people, some just starting college, are becoming more knowledgeable and interested in these very things. I think there is going to be a big movement over the next ten years or so that might shake things up," Rita predicted.

Sheriff Williams of Seward County, Kansas, was excited. On the phone to Sheriff Edwardo Sisneros he said, "You're not going to believe what I found."

"What's that?" Ed asked.

"I finally tracked down the Cimino family. They moved to Garden City, Kansas, and I went there to interview them. While I was visiting with them I was wandering around their living room, looking at pictures and so forth, when I noticed a photo on the mantle of their daughter in her high school prom dress with a fellow known as Jim Lackey. It definitely is a picture of the woman you are investigating for Lackey's murder, and without a doubt it is Jim Lackey in the photo."

I asked the Ciminos about the picture and they told me their daughter Anne had gone to the prom with Lackey. They said she then went to Lamar, Colorado, where she dated a Sean Sullivan in college. She had even brought him home one time for Christmas when the parents lived in Liberal. Sean seemed like a nice young man with very good manners. They also remembered when Lackey worked at the bank in Liberal. I asked them if their daughter had any contact with Lackey while she was visiting them, and they didn't know but didn't think so," Sheriff Williams related.

"This is a huge breakthrough," Sheriff Sisneros declared. "You have done a fantastic job of gathering this background."

"I have an interest is this case, too. I want to clear up our cold case, and I think we are a lot closer to doing just that. My theory, if you're interested, is that Anne and Sean met Lackey by chance while they were here for Christmas in 1950, maybe at a restaurant or coffee shop. Lackey proposed they join him in a scheme to rob the bank. Maybe the thrill of it all appealed to them and they agreed to do it. There was probably a lot of planning involved and they waited for a signal from Lackey that there was a lot of cash in the bank. In January of 1951 they did the deed, met up at a designated spot to split the loot, burned the car, and everyone went their own way," Sheriff Williams surmised.

"Sounds plausible to me," Ed said. "Then Sean and Anne went back to college as if nothing had happened."

"If it ever does all play out and we learn the truth, I bet that theory is pretty close to what occurred."

"That may be, but now we have to prove it. Our office will work on that. Thanks once again for all your help. This information is extremely important and gives us more to go on. Please send that picture and any other information you have to my office. I appreciate it," Sheriff

Sisneros said signing off.

Doug was riding through the cow pastures one mid-March day when there was a high pressure weather system over southern Colorado, making it a very pleasant fifty-degree day. The cows were grazing on some leftover grass from last year and plucking an occasional green sprig. The calves were running and playing and having a good time. The snow was melting and the ground was soaking it up. Suddenly Doug stopped his horse and looked up into the sky, listening for a familiar sound that would guide his eyes. Sure enough, high overhead was a vee-shaped flock of Canada geese heading north. "It won't be long now," he mused, thinking of spring, green grass, and an end to winter's icy grip on the land.

BC, who had also heard the sound, was looking up to see where it was coming from. He seemed to agree with Doug that it was time for warmer weather.

"These cold winters are getting harder to take every year, aren't they ol' pard?" Doug said to BC, who wagged his tail in agreement.

Doug was riding a new young horse he had been working with during the winter. The horse was of the same stock as Dunny and Frog Honey, and he showed a lot of interest in cattle. Doug would let him select a cow to start pushing slowing along, relaxing the reins and resting his hands on the saddle horn while the horse made all the decisions. The colt proved to be a natural in cutting—moving one particular animal out of a herd—and working cattle. Some horses were bred for this and really loved their work.

As he finished up with "horse school" for the day and started heading back toward camp, he noticed his boss, Dub, riding a horse about a half mile off. He headed over to jaw awhile with Dub.

"Hey Dub, I see you're riding a young horse too," Doug greeted. "How's the schooling going?"

"It's going very well. This colt is related to the one you're riding. They sure show a lot of cow sense," Dub answered excitedly.

Nothing got Dub's interest up like a good horse. He loved them, especially cow horses. His theory was that God had created the cow for one purpose only—to give the horse something to do.

"I'm glad I got a chance to see you. I've been meaning to talk to you and Fro and John. The folks who own the Circle Cross Ranch have an opportunity to purchase a property in New Mexico and they want to know if any of us would be willing to move there to help run it," Dub explained.

"Wow, that is surprising news. When is this going to happen?" Doug asked.

"They are in negotiations now. They will probably sell this place, and they have offers from several different sources to sell it piecemeal. It could be within the next few months or it could take a year," Dub stated.

"What's the ranch in New Mexico like? Is it decent cow country?" Doug asked, like a true cowboy who always wants to know whether a new range can support cattle.

"It's better cow country than this is. It's perfect for a mama cow operation, which is what the owners want. There's a lot of high summer pasture and also lower country that's excellent winter pasture. The snow and winters aren't as bad there, so there isn't as much winter feeding required. There's about a hundred and twenty thousand acres, all of them deeded, which will carry about thirty five hundred units under normal conditions. Plus there is a lot of wildlife to support a fishing and hunting program," Dub answered.

"Where is the ranch located—what part of New Mexico?"

"It's a neighbor to Bear Mountain Scout Ranch in Colfax County near Cimarron."

"That's where Rita used to work. Steve Sheldon works at Bear Mountain," Doug offered.

"Yeah, I know. So what do you think? Would you be willing to move?" Dub asked.

"Are you going? I'd be more inclined to move if I knew you were gonna be my boss."

"Well, I appreciate the vote of confidence. Yes, Polly and I talked it over and we are excited about making the move."

"I'll have to talk it over with Rita, but I'm sure she would love to get back to that country. That's where she was headed when I interrupted her plans. I don't want to get my hopes up too much about this. How certain is it?" Doug asked.

"The purchase of the New Mexico ranch is almost a sure thing. The owners don't even have to borrow the money. They have the cash. I expect that part of it will happen fairly soon," Dub answered.

"We have some good friends here that we would hate to

leave, but I think I would like to see what's over the next mountain," Doug said.

"You're a typical cowboy. Always ready to roll you're bed and head on down the trail," Dub laughed.

Doug hurried home to tell Rita the news, and she received it with equal excitement. After supper they talked for hours about the possible move.

A grand jury hearing was held in Walsenburg during which the jurors decided that, even though the evidence against Angela and Sean was circumstantial, it was compelling enough to go to trial. The judge decided to continue bail for both defendants. A few days later Mr. Salazar called the DA to asked if a meeting could be set up to discuss a plea agreement. The DA was curious so he agreed to meet with them the following week.

The next day Mr. Frederici called with the same request. The DA arranged to talk with all of the parties at the same meeting, and they gathered the following Wednesday in the DA's office with a court recorder present.

"You all called the meeting. What's this about?" the DA asked.

"We would like to know if a plea bargain would be possible. Would you take first degree murder off the table in exchange for a lesser charge, if Miss Cimino allocutes?" Mr. Salazar opened the discussion.

"We were wondering the same thing," Mr. Frederici said.

"That depends on what your clients have to say," Mr. Stevens, the DA, responded. "Let's hear it."

"We need some assurances that you will consider a plea

agreement," Mr. Salazar stated.

"What were you hoping for? How far down do you want me to go? They're not going to get a free ride," Mr. Stevens said.

"How about manslaughter? My client was under extreme duress," Mr. Salazar explained.

"I don't know anything about duress. Your client hasn't exactly been forthcoming throughout this whole business," the DA stated emphatically.

"You have to understand that my client was in fear for her life. She did not come forward because she didn't want to involve Mr. Sullivan here or her family," Mr. Salazar answered.

"Okay, let's hear the story."

"Off the record?"

"Yeah, okay," Mr. Stevens said, signaling the recorder to turn off the machine.

"Lackey was terrorizing me," Angela or Anne began her story. "I met him in high school. He was one of those guys who is always pestering girls, and the girls thought he was disgusting. I had a terrible inferiority complex at that time and didn't think anyone was going to ask me to the prom, so I agreed to go with him. He had been so persistent, and my father thought it was wonderful. My father was very strict, but a terrible judge of human character. So I went with Jim."

"After the prom he drove me out to the country, despite my insistence that he take me home. He tried to rape me. I fought like a tiger and he became violent and enraged.

I told him that I was going to tell my father, so he finally took me home. I told my mother what happened but never told my father because I was afraid he would be angry at me. I never wanted anything to do with Lackey after that and avoided him everywhere I went."

"I got a college scholarship at Lamar State, where I met Sean. I liked him but he was very shy and so was I, so we didn't start dating until our junior year. I fell in love with him. He is so unlike other young men I've met. He is kind and very gentle—he is the love of my life," she said looking at Sean, smiling.

Sean was looking at Anne and said, "I love you, too."

"I invited Sean to go home with me one Christmas to meet my parents," Anne continued. "All went well. My parents liked him and he liked them. Then one day we were in downtown Liberal and went to the bank to cash a check when the teller was none other than Lackey. He was very personable and invited us to go for coffee with him. I was hesitant, but Sean, being the nice guy he is, thought it would be fine."

"While at coffee Lackey took us into his confidence and told us about his scheme for robbing the bank. At first I thought he was joking, but he kept telling us it was foolproof and that he wanted us to help him. At first when we discussed it we almost decided to go to the sheriff and tell him the whole story. I wish now that we had. Over the next couple of weeks we talked about it, and Sean was tempted because he really needed money. Bankers were about to take his family's ranch from them, so we decided to do it."

"We called Lackey and told him we were in. He was elated and made arrangements to meet us at a town halfway between Liberal and Lamar so we could make plans. We met him, laid out the plans, and even decided where to go afterward to split the money. He said he would call us and let us know when the job was to be done, because they were expecting a lot of money to come into the bank in the next couple of weeks."

"It went off without a hitch. We escaped in an old sedan that Lackey provided, went to the place in the Oklahoma panhandle where we were supposed to meet, and waited for him. In a couple of hours he showed up, we split the money three ways, set fire to the car, and Sean and I went back to Lamar. I was terrified because I thought the police were going to show up at any moment and arrest us."

"Sean used his share to pay off the note on his ranch. I put my share in an old military ammo box that Sean gave me and hid it. I couldn't bear to use any of it, and over time it became a huge weight on my conscience. As the years went by and no law enforcement people showed up, we thought we had gotten away with it."

"Then one day I saw Lackey. I was supposed to meet Sean in a cantina in Trinidad and was waiting for him when Lackey sat down at my table. I was so shocked I almost passed out. He kept insisting that he wanted to get back together with me, but I never wanted to see him again. About that time Sean showed up and told Lackey not to contact us anymore."

"He must have found out where I lived because he showed up at the library in La Veta one day. I was very frightened and didn't know what to do. He wanted to have sex with me and said if I didn't he would tell the authorities that I was responsible for the robbery. I told Sean what was going on, of course, and he was outraged and wanted to hunt Lackey down and have it out with him. I talked him out of that. I was meeting Sean at one of the vacant cow camps on the Circle Cross ranch once in a while. I was a little paranoid and thought we should be discreet. Evidently Lackey followed me or somehow found out where we were meeting and showed up there one day."

"I was still on my horse and he kept insisting that I join him in the house. I spurred my horse and nearly ran him over, riding off in a panic up the trail behind the corrals. He followed me in his truck but was pulling a horse trailer, so he finally had to stop and get his horse out to pursue me on horseback. I thought I was safe after a while, but when I looked back he was still there, so I just kept going up the mountain."

"The trail I was on came out into a grassy meadow. I didn't know where I was or what I was going to do. I just knew I had to get away from him. At the upper end of this grassy meadow was a canyon, and I followed a dim trail up the gorge. My little paint mare was getting very tired so I stopped to let her rest, and that's when he caught up to me. He was so full of himself, laughing and saying I had picked out the perfect spot where no one would see us."

"He got hold of me and began ripping at my clothes. I was desperate and fighting as hard as I could. He knocked me to the ground and was crouching over me when I picked up a rock and hit him in the face with it. He staggered back, but became enraged and told me how he was going to make me pay for that. Suddenly there was a very loud boom and Lackey went flying back into some tree limbs that were lying in the bottom of the canyon. I turned around to look, and Sean was standing there with his rifle in his hand. Sean told me to get on my horse and get out of there immediately."

Angela paused, and the DA asked, "Is that it? Is there anything else you need to tell us?"

"I think that's everything. I'm willing to work with you, so if you have any more questions, just ask," she answered.

"Let's hear from you, Mr. Sullivan. Do you have anything to add to what Miss Cimino had to say?"

"Yes. Anne had nothing to do with the killing—that was all on me. When I arrived at the cow camp that day I could tell by the tracks what had happened, so I followed as far as I could in my pickup and horse trailer. When I got to where Lackey had parked his vehicle, I followed on horseback. I had my black powder rifle on the gun rack in my truck, so I put it in the scabbard on the saddle before mounting up. It was easy to follow their tracks, and I hurried as fast as my horse would go."

"When I caught up I saw what Lackey was trying to do to Anne and a rage came over me. I pulled out my rifle, made sure it was charged, and shot him in the chest. The blast of the fifty caliber blew him back into that deadfall. I then told Anne to get out of there. After she left I picked up his rifle, fired all the cartridges into a dirt, and in a rage used the stock to bash his head in. I untied his horse, took off its bridle and turned it loose, and caught up with Anne in a couple of miles."

"We agreed not to say anything to anyone. I figured that if it was a while before anyone found the body, they would think the death was caused by wild animals. Also it was the rainy season and I was hoping the rain would wipe out all the sign," Sean stated.

"Your plan almost worked," the DA said. "If it weren't for a smart cowboy and deputy, and the forensics experts, you would have gotten away with it."

"So what can you do for us?" both lawyers wanted to know.

"How about murder two with recommendations at sentencing?" the DA inquired.

"How about manslaughter?" Mr. Salazar asked.

"I don't think so," answered the DA. "After all there was some premeditation here. I could go for murder one."

"Then you'll never get the confession on record and you're right back to circumstantial evidence," Mr. Frederici advised.

"Let me discuss this with my colleagues and I'll get back to you," the DA stated, ending the meeting.

The excitement and anticipation of moving to another ranch affected everyone who worked on the Circle Cross. Dub went to see John and Sonja Latham to discuss the possibility of them moving also. John was thrilled to be asked, but Sonja was a little more reserved. She had a good job with the school system and she wasn't sure John was ready to take on the strenuous work required of a ranch hand. To prove otherwise, John invited them outside to his corral where he caught a horse, saddled it, and with a mighty effort mounted and rode around a bit.

"I'm getting stronger every day. I'll be ready," he proudly stated. "Besides, Sonja, there ain't no grizzly's in that country."

"Let's hope not, anyway," Dub said.

Doug was riding back to Echo camp one evening after a day of checking cows and moving cattle into different pastures in preparation for the official count that the new owners would make. They were buying not only the land but the buildings, equipment, rolling stock, and livestock—except for the riding horses. Most of those horses were of a distinct line of American Quarter Horse that was selectively bred for a hundred years with "cow sense." This line of horses was considered more valuable than the cattle. They were particularly adept at cutting and sorting cattle, and were prized by enthusiasts all over the West.

Doug hoped to make it back home about the same time as Rita, who had gone to see her doctor to make sure all was well with the pregnancy. She knew everything was okay, but went anyway to satisfy Doug who was like an old mother hen. When he arrived at Echo camp, Rita wasn't back home yet so he decided to ride out into the horse trap that was up the bench to the west of the camp and bring in all the horses. He wanted to give them a good brushing, check their shoes, and get them ready for the trip.

As he went through the gate into the horse trap he noticed someone else had been through the gate. By the looks of the tracks he was fairly sure it was Angela. With wrinkled brow he wondered what she was doing there. As he was riding along following Angela's tracks he noticed another horse track.

> "Now that looks like Lackey's horse track. What the hell is going on here?" he asked BC, who was as dumbfounded as Doug.

As they followed the tracks they approached the rim of the canyon. Soon Doug found where the two horses had been tied to a cedar tree about a hundred feet from the rim. On the ground under the tree was a saddle, saddle pads, and a bridle that Doug recognized from Angela's stable when he had gone there a few months ago. Doug tied up his own horse and proceeded on foot. It was so rocky and gravelly that it was difficult to find any footprints, but occasionally he could see the edge of a boot print or a disturbed pebble that indicated someone had walked this way. When he stepped on a large flat rock on the edge of the rim, a bunch of magpies flew up from the bottom of the canyon. Looking at the spot where they scattered, he saw a splash of what appeared to be bright colored cloth.

He and BC began climbing down through the boulders and the oak brush until he figured he was close to the spot. He stopped, began looking around, and suddenly caught a smell—a smell that he knew all too well—a smell that brought back memories of his time in the Korean War. War is hell in so many ways, but one of the worst is the smells and how they are indelibly imprinted on your mind.

Knowing what he would find, he began searching and found a body a few yards away, lying in a thicket of brush among several boulders. He scanned the body closely enough to determine for sure that it was Angela. Looking around to see if there was anything else of interest, and looking up at the rim to estimate the spot from which the body had probably dropped, he said, "Come on, BC, there is nothing else we can do here." Doug placed his coat over the top part of the body, and made the long climb up to the edge of the cliff.

After arriving at Echo camp and seeing that Rita was home, he put up his horse and went to tell her what he had discovered.

"We have to go to headquarters and phone Harlan."

On the way Rita told him that the doctor had given her a clean bill of health and all was well with her and the baby.

"He also thinks I'm a little further along than what I thought. We may have to name it *Bunkhouse Surprise*, if you know what I mean," she said.

"I know exactly what you mean," Doug answered.

When they got to headquarters he found Dub in the office along with Fro. Doug explained to them what he had found.

"Fro, is Lackey's horse still at your camp?" Doug asked.

"No, Lackey's wife came and got it a couple of weeks ago. I had pulled its shoes and turned it out in the horse trap," Fro answered.

"I called her and told her she needed to come and get it," Dub said, "That we were leaving and the horse had eaten all the free grass it was going to get."

"Why do you ask?" Fro inquired.

"I don't know. I saw a horse track in the Echo camp horse trap that looked like that horse's hoof. It's got me buffaloed. Well, I need to call Harlan," Doug answered.

When Harlan got the news, he was at home since it was late in the day. His first reaction was, "What? You found what? Don't move—I'm on my way out—where are you?"

"We're at headquarters in Dub's office. We'll stay right here," Doug answered.

Harlan arrived less than an hour later and came into the office with his eyes full of questions. "Now tell me everything."

"I found Angela in Echo Canyon today—dead. It looks like she went off the rim and fell about eighty feet into a pile of brush and rocks below. I didn't examine her enough to tell how she died. I covered her some to keep the magpies off her," Doug answered sadly.

Harlan immediately got on the phone to the sheriff's office and reported what Doug had told him.

"I bet it was Sully—do you think it was Sully, Doug? Or maybe she jumped to commit suicide?" Harlan was scrambling for answers.

"I think you need to see the scene in the daylight. I also have some horse tracks I need to show you," Doug said. "Plus, I now have an extra horse in my horse trap. Whoever was up there with Angela unsaddled her horse and turned it lose."

"Oh, you and your horse tracks... What did you find?" Harlan asked reluctantly.

"I found Angela's horse's tracks and also what I think are Lackey's unshod horse's tracks," Doug answered. "Also Angela's saddle and bridle."

"What? This gets more confusing all the time," Harlan replied. "Right now you need to take me to where the body is. I'll radio the team and tell them where to come."

When they arrived at Echo camp Doug unlocked the gate at the county road so all the sheriff's department vehicles could get through. Polly and Rita went to the house to make coffee and sandwiches for all the people who would be there most of the night. Harlan, Fro, Dub, and Doug gathered in the yard waiting for the rest of the sheriff's department and the forensic team.

"Before you let a bunch of vehicles in the horse trap you need to remember there are some tracks you may want to preserve," Doug stated.

"Can they drive to the canyon rim?" Harlan asked.

"Yes, with a four-wheel-drive vehicle. I put all the horses

in the corral so we can leave the gate open, but first I want you to see these tracks over here by the gate," Doug said, leading the way.

They all proceeded to the gate and Doug pointed out the tracks of the horses that had gone through the gate recently.

About that time Sheriff Sisneros arrived and they discussed everything with him. Shortly, another sheriff's department unit arrived followed by the coroner. Harlan provided the briefing for the team.

"Everyone follow my vehicle. Doug is going to ride with me and direct me so that we don't drive on top of the physical evidence in the form of tracks. Everyone carry flashlights and make sure of where you are stepping so as not to step on existing tracks."

The vehicles proceeded in single file to the rim several yards down the canyon from where Doug had found the body. All of the Circle Cross cowboys had piled into Harlan's unit in case they were needed to help bring the body out. As it turned out they were needed because, after a disgruntled coroner made it to the body and did his examination, he wanted it loaded on a litter and hauled up to the rim. It took all the cowboys and several sheriff's deputies to accomplish this feat.

The body was loaded into the coroner's vehicle, and after making a careful search of the area, everyone returned to the Echo camp yard where Rita invited them inside for coffee and sandwiches. Some of the overweight deputies were the first to accept this invitation. After everyone left, Rita and Doug were finally able to get to bed in the wee hours of the morning, knowing it was going to be a short night because Harlan he said he would be back early the next day.

Doug was grumbling when he got into bed.

"What's with you?" Rita asked.

"Sometimes I feel like trading my bedroll for a lantern, as hard as it is to get any sleep around this place," he groused. All Rita could do was laugh at him.

"You think it's bad now, wait until the little one is here and you have to get up for those three AM feedings," she said.

"Just stick a tit in its mouth—it'll be fine," Doug said, pulling the covers up to his chin and snuggling up to Rita.

Harlan was back the next morning and went with Doug to get some plaster casts of several horse and human tracks. He also thoroughly searched the area on top of the rim and down in the canyon where the body was found, but he could not find any additional evidence.

"I thought sure it would prove to be Sully, but as it turns out he has an alibi for the time when she was killed. I also thought it might be suicide, but now I have my doubts," Harlan shared with Doug.

"I don't think it was suicide. I think there was someone else up here when it happened. What worries me is that other set of horse tracks. Somebody was here, maybe not at the same time but probably close. Also, the tracks look like Lackey's horse," Doug offered.

"The horse track you and I saw was unshod. You can't tell what horse made those tracks."

"Maybe *si*, maybe *no*. Fro also thought they were from Lackey's horse," Doug said.

"We have plaster casts of the tracks. Maybe they will prove that you are correct. Right now I think I'm going to pay a little visit to Lackey's wife," Harlan said.

"When you do, take some backup. If she did this, then she is capable of anything," Doug advised.

The next day Harlan went to Walsenburg to talk to Mrs. Lackey again. On the way the sheriff called on the radio to ask him to come by his office first. When Harlan arrived the sheriff said,

"Let's walk over to the DA's office. He wants to see us."

Upon entering the office the DA asked, "How is the case going? What are the latest developments?"

"It appears that Sullivan did not kill his girlfriend. We have evidence that someone else was up there with her when it happened. Did you receive the forensic report as to cause of death?" Harlan asked the sheriff.

"Yes, it was not suicide. There was a bullet hole in the back of the head, covered up by the hair. You probably didn't see it during your preliminary exam. The bullet was a twenty-two with no exit wound," the sheriff answered.

"My friend, the cowboy, that's been so helpful in the investigation of this case is certain there was another person up there with Miss Cimino the day she was killed. His theory is based on horse tracks. In fact, he thinks he knows the horse that made the tracks. He thinks it was Lackey's horse," Harlan offered.

"Lackey's horse—how is that possible?" the DA asked.

"Lackey's wife picked up that horse from the Circle Cross only two weeks ago. It's possible she trailered the horse back up there to confront Miss Cimino. She may have forced her to ride to the canyon rim, where she killed the victim," Harlan theorized.

"Do you have any evidence to back this up, or is this another cowboy hunch?" the DA inquired.

"No evidence—I was on my way to question Mrs. Lackey when the sheriff called me to come here," Harlan stated.

"Don't go there by yourself. I'll go with you," said Sheriff Sisneros.

"All right. Off with you two, and let me know what you find out," the DA ordered.

When they arrived at Mrs. Lackey's house they went to the front and Harlan rapped on the door. After trying two or three more times, the sheriff said,

"I'll go round back." In a few minutes he returned, saying, "Don't appear to be anyone home."

About that time a neighbor lady pushing a cart laden with groceries passed the entrance to the Lackey driveway. When she paused to see what was going on, Harlan walked over to her.

"Do you know if Mrs. Lackey is at home?"

"I don't think she is. I saw her loading clothes and other stuff in her pickup a few days ago. She had a horse trailer hitched to the back of the pickup with a brown horse in it," the lady said.

"When was this?" the sheriff asked as he walked up to them.

"I'm pretty sure it was three days ago," she answered.

"Thank you," Harlan said. "Let me get your name, address, and phone number in case we need to contact you again."

In the meantime the sheriff returned to the vehicle, calling his office on the radio to ask the Motor Vehicle Department for the license number of Mrs. Lackey's vehicle. He ordered an all-points bulletin to have her found and detained.

"She could be anywhere by now," Harlan offered. "I'm going to do a background check to see if she has any family nearby."

While they were in the neighborhood they questioned the other neighbors, but no one knew very much about the Lackey's or where they had come from. Harlan and Sheriff Sisneros also went to the bar where Mrs. Lackey worked and talked to her employer, checking her employment records. After they returned to the courthouse Harlan called the sheriff in Liberal, Kansas, to see if Lackey's wife may have been from the same area as her husband. He also alerted them to be on the lookout for her in case she showed up in that part of the country.

Sheriff Sisneros informed the DA that their new suspect had done a runner. The DA briefed the sheriff that they had heard from Sean Sullivan's lawyer, and that Sean was willing to plead guilty to manslaughter in the killing of Lackey. According to the lawyer, Sean was terribly depressed over the death of Anne Cimino and just wanted to put all the legal proceedings behind him. The DA advised the sheriff that if the judge agreed to this plea, it would be the best solution to that case. They could then concentrate their efforts on catching the killer of Anne Cimino.

In the first part of May a huge going-away party was held in the American Legion hall at La Veta for all the Circle Cross employees who were leaving the area. All of the "due diligence," inventories, herd counts, and other requirements for the bean counters were completed. Everyone would be moving during the next few days. Harlan, Celeste, Doug, and Rita were sitting at the same table.

"We sure are going to miss you guys," Celeste said wistfully.

"I know—we are going to miss you all, too," Rita said with a catch in her voice. She and Celeste had become very good friends in the few months since they had known each other.

"Doesn't mean we can't see each other once in a while. When you get your vacations, bring your kids and stay with us for a while. We would love to have you," Doug said.

"Sounds like a good idea to me," Harlan added. "As long

as I stay here I can't get away from work. Even when I'm on vacation people are always calling me for something."

"That's because you have spoiled them," Celeste said.

"Look who's talking! You never refuse anyone," Harlan volleyed.

"That's what the Lord wants us to do—help each other," Celeste replied with a twinkle in her eye.

"I know, and you are one of his best angels," Harlan finally conceded.

"I'll drink to that," Doug chimed in, raising his bottle of beer.

"Hear, hear," Rita sang out, as they all clinked beer bottles.

"Hey, I have something for you," Harlan said, handing a picture of Lackey's wife taken from her DMV photo, "just in case you run across her in your travels."

"I'm sure I've seen her before, but I can't remember where," Doug said looking at the picture. "Anyway, I hope you get this whole mess figured out. When you do, let us know. I'm curious as to how it's going to end."

In the next few days there was a caravan of pickups pulling horse trailers, hauling horses and household goods, back and forth between the Colorado ranch and the New Mexico ranch. Late one evening Doug and Rita pulled into Cimarron, New Mexico, and stopped at the St. James Hotel where they decided to stay the night. The house at the camp where they would be living was not ready for habitation. According to Rita it needed a thorough cleaning and some painting. Almost all of the camps were the same, as Polly put it—they looked like a bunch of cowboys had been living in them.

Doug and Rita had already moved all the horses, so on this trip they had household goods. It wouldn't hurt to leave the stuff in the horse trailer overnight. After checking into the hundred-year-old hotel and getting settled in their room, they decided to go to the dining room for supper. This old hotel had been around during Cimarron's seedier past. It had seen many gunfights and had a reputation for being a wild place many years ago.

It even harbored a ghost in one of its rooms, or so the current owners claimed. Supposedly a card game was going on in an upstairs room late one night when one of the participants thought he had been cheated. He staggered across the hall to his room and fetched his gun, returning to the game to shoot the suspected cheater. There was an exchange of gunfire and the cowboy returned to his room. The next morning he was found dead and, as the story goes, his ghost inhabits that room to this day.

Rita and Doug settled at one of the dining room tables and ordered enchiladas and beer. Looking into the bar adjacent to the dining room, Rita said,

"That's her!"

"That's who?" Doug asked.

"Where is that picture Harlan gave you?"

"It's in the room with our luggage."

"Doesn't that look like the person in that picture—the gal sitting on the stool at the bar?"

When Doug glanced up, the woman was looking back at him with some recognition in her eyes.

"Yeah, that's her all right," Doug said. "I think she saw

us staring at her. She's leaving. Should I follow her to see where she goes?"

"No, you should stay right here and eat your supper, and we'll call Harlan when we get back to the room," Rita advised.

"You saw her!" Harlan said excitedly after answering the phone at his house. "Does she know you saw her?"

"Yes, I'm sure she recognized me because she left there immediately," Doug answered. "I asked the bartender and waitress if they knew her, but no one knew anything about her. Do you want me to get in touch with the local law?"

"No, I'll do that. I may have to come over there in the next day or two," Harlan advised.

"Good—you can stay with us. We'll have our house ready before too long," Doug said signing off.

"That's easy for you to say," Rita remarked after Doug hung up the phone. "We have a lot of work to do on that house before we move in, so we'd better get to bed and get an early start tomorrow morning."

"Yes, ma'am," Doug replied.

He was already learning what every husband must learn—a happy wife is a happy home. If the husband doesn't learn this unwritten law, or opts to fight it with his own brand of machismo, there is hell to pay and he will never find happiness.

Harlan got in touch with the sheriff's office in Colfax County located in Raton, New Mexico. He explained that a person of interest involved in a murder in Huerfano County,

Colorado, may have fled to their jurisdiction. He also sent copies of the suspect's picture to their office. The representative of the Colfax County Sheriff's Department that resided in Cimarron, New Mexico, was a pretty Latina named Beatrix Rodriquez. She was 5' 4", slight of frame, with a very cute figure, black hair and eyes. She had been a deputy about ten years and was currently just thirty-two years old.

Beatrix had spent the first four years at the department working in the county jail, the place where all rookie deputies must start. Her stint there may have been protracted due to the fact that she was a woman working in what was normally an all-male occupation. The verbal and sexual abuse she sustained there, from coworkers and prisoners alike, only steeled her resolve to stick it out and make a successful career in law enforcement. Her abilities and determination won her the admiration of most of her colleagues. She studied and received a degree in law enforcement at the University of New Mexico, and she had been stationed in Cimarron for the past four years.

Beatrix, known by nearly everyone as Betty or B-Rod, received the information from Harlan a few days after he sent it. She immediately called Harlan to learn all the details. Armed with this background and the photos, she proceeded to search for the elusive Mrs. Lackey. Betty found out that Nora Lackey had stayed at the Kit Carson Inn but suddenly left a few days before. She had kept a horse at a local boarding stable, and a short time after checking out of the motel she loaded her horse in a trailer and departed.

There didn't seem to be anyone in town who had an extended conversation with Mrs. Lackey while she was in Cimarron, except the bartender at the St. James. He claimed that she had "come on to him" and was looking for a job as a bartender or waitress. Their relationship never progressed beyond this, so he didn't know anything else about her. The owner of the stable thought she might have gone west on US highway 64 when she left town.

Betty's jurisdiction extended west to the Taos County line, marked by a ridge of mountains on the far side of Moreno Valley west of Eagle Nest and Angel Fire. Betty was due to make her regular appearance in that area, so the next morning she drove there, checking Ute Park on the way. At the local watering hole in Eagle Nest one of the regulars thought he remembered seeing the woman in the photo. It was a few days earlier when this woman came in and had a beer. Knowing the woman was traveling with a horse, Betty checked local boarding stables but came up empty.

She then proceeded to Angel Fire and found a boarding stable whose operator remembered the woman and the horse, which he had boarded for one night. Betty stopped at a convenience store and was showing the picture to the employees when a deputy from Taos County came in for some refreshments. Betty visited with the Taos deputy and gave him copies of the picture and information.

She then traveled through the community of Angel Fire and began checking the bars. At one of the ski lodge bars she hit pay dirt. The bartender, a middle-aged lady who identified herself as the regular day shift bartender, said the woman in the photo had been there two days before. Since the place had been empty at the time, she and the woman had an extended conversation.

Betty asked if the woman said anything about where she was staying, where she had come from, or where she was going. The bartender said she remembered the woman saying she was from Colorado, but assumed she was just passing through. The lady bartender said the woman had stayed in the bar a couple of hours or so, and when the bar started filling up with other people she lost track of her. She recalled that the lady sat at a table with one of the regulars, Tony

Garcia, who had a small ranch somewhere south of there. She didn't know whether they left together.

Betty went back to the stable where Mrs. Lackey had boarded the horse and asked the manager if he had seen anyone with Mrs. Lackey when she picked up the horse. He couldn't remember seeing anyone with her. When asked if he knew a Tony Garcia, he said he thought Tony was a rancher down south by Guadalapito or maybe Ocate. As it was getting late, Betty decided to go back to Cimarron and do some research from her office the following day.

As it turned out she would not able to get back to this case because there were several full days ahead. She had to investigate a case of shoplifting at one of the stores in Cimarron—there was a fight at the high school between some exuberant young males with an overabundance of testosterone—a small ranch owner reported a missing cow—and of course she had obligations for traffic patrol on the highway through town. It was several days before Betty had time to do more research from her office.

Doug and Rita finally got settled into their house at Rayado camp. Doug was chomping at the bit to ride the new country he was responsible for, but first he had to make sure mama was happy. He hoped Dub was not too disappointed in him, but he found out that Dub was going through the same thing. One morning Doug told Rita that he had to go check fences. He waited uneasily for her response, but she looked at him, smiled, and told him to go ahead. She knew full well that there are some interior decorating chores where a man's presence is best used elsewhere.

Doug sent BC out to gather the horses, who were getting fat and lazy from not being rode for a spell. He caught and saddled Frog Honey, who seemed eager for a ride. They trotted down to the cookhouse first to see if Hugh Gillespie was around. Hugh was an eighty-something-year-old cowhand who had worked on this ranch for about forty years. Doug knew Hugh would be able to tell him whatever he wanted to know about the layout of the ranch, the fences, the cattle, or anything else.

Hugh was in his saddle barn working on a bridle. One

thing Doug knew about Hugh was that a person had to make sure he was upwind from him. He always had a chaw of Red Man tobacco in his cheek and wasn't too careful when and where he spit. Hugh had once been about five foot ten when he stood up straight, but all the years of hard ranch life, along with a lot of wrecks on bad horses, had taken their toll on his old bones. He was stooped over and shuffled rather than walked, but he was up every morning before the crack of dawn, had his coffee, went to the barn to call his horses where he fed, curried, and fussed over them. Then he'd select the one he was going to ride that day.

Since he led his life very frugally, including the way he ate, he didn't weigh one hundred thirty-five pounds soaking wet. Besides the ever-present chaw, he always wore an old cowboy hat that looked like it had been through a war. It was about the same color as the dirt on the ground, if that dirt had a little horse dung mixed in with it. There wasn't even a clue as to what its original color was. Hugh always wore jeans, boots, and a denim shirt which all looked very worn. Under this he wore one-piece long johns, winter and summer. The outer wear was a very old pair of leggins, spurs, and a Levi jacket—the front of which was covered with tobacco spittle.

Hugh actually had two Levi jackets. One he wore every morning, because it was usually a bit brisk early in the morning in this part of the country. The other he called his "new one," even though his daughter had given it to him for Christmas twenty years before. He used that one as a pillow. He slept in a side room of the cookhouse on a narrow army cot. He used the same bedroll that he had slept in forever, and even he couldn't remember how long he'd had that bedroll. Hopefully he'd washed it once in a while during that time.

Hugh was very wizened and stove up, but he was able to get on his horse every morning. His usual routine was to check fences, and he carried on his saddle some fencing pliers and almost everything he needed to make simple repairs. He checked every fence within ten miles of Rayado camp at least every two weeks. Every once in a while the ramrod would have him do some other chore. When cattle were on their winter feed grounds he would ride through them every couple of days to make sure they were okay. Dub had met with Hugh after taking over as ramrod and reassured him his duties wouldn't change. This was a relief to Hugh, because he had convinced himself he would probably be let go. No one wanted to hire the elderly anymore.

Doug found out from Hugh what fences had been checked, which ones might need repair in the near future, what the grass looked like, and how the cattle looked. Hugh suggested the "cattle drive" might need to be checked as he had not rode up that high all winter. The "cattle drive" was a trail that went to the high country. It was fenced on each side about one hundred yards wide, and it ran from a lower pasture up over a rim that was at least a thousand feet higher and was about three or four miles long.

After the spring roundup the gates at the bottom and the top of the drive were opened so the cattle could travel from the low country to the high country. Some old mama cows would look for the open gates on their own, but most had to be driven by cowboys. This high country pasture was about twenty thousand acres in size and was from eight thousand feet to well over ten thousand feet in altitude. It had three high country lakes that were a trout fisherman's delight. There were several other high country pastures on the ranch, some on top of mesas that required very little fencing because the rims were so steep that cattle would not attempt to go over them. There was a bulldozed trail cut in the rim in one or two places that allowed access up to these mesa-top pastures.

Doug was in awe as he rode across the ranch. This range was all new to him, and he couldn't get over what beautiful scenery there was and what good cow country it was. He was acquainting himself with the lay of the land and took in all his surroundings. BC was enjoying it too as he discovered a myriad of new smells—deer, elk, bear, and even different kinds of cats who left trails to sniff. Doug rode up the "cattle drive" trail, finding the fences in good shape, except for the gate at the top. It was lying in a tangled heap in the fence opening. The elk had been using this trail too, and they trampled the gate wires so many times that they finally tore the gate down and left it in a mess.

For some unexplained reason elk, when jumping a fence, always hit the top wire with their front and back feet. If you're down the fence line from where a bunch of elk are crossing, you can hear the wires singing from them tapping the top wire. Many times this repeated striking of the wire will cause it to break. When this happens and as they continue to cross at the same spot, they will strike the second wire down and so on. Rarely do elk get tangled in the fence, but when it happens they usually get free. Doug had only ever found one dead elk that had gotten tangled in a fence.

He didn't have the necessary equipment with him to fix the gate, so he made a mental note to return with a four-wheel vehicle and fix it later. Doug rode far enough into the high country pasture to come out into a large open park. The grass was beginning to get green in spots, even though there was still a lot of snow in the trees. At the far end of the park a large herd of elk was grazing, and when they saw the man, horse, and dog, they eased into the timber slowly without looking too concerned.

When Betty finally had a chance to check out Tony Garcia she consulted with the Motor Vehicle Department and with the Sheriff's Department of Mora County. She obtained an address and phone number of a Tony Garcia who had a ranch between Ocate and Black Lakes. When she called the number a woman answered.

"This is Deputy Betty Rodriquez of Colfax County. Is Tony Garcia there?" Betty asked.

"What do you want Tony for?" the woman asked nervously.

"I just need to talk to him. Are you his wife?"

"No. Can I give him a message?"

"Please have him call me when he gets in," Betty said giving the woman the phone number.

After they had both disconnected, Betty sat thinking. "I bet that is the woman I'm searching for", and she called Harlan's office to leave a message apprising him of what she discovered. The next morning Harlan called Betty just as she was preparing to leave the office.

"Do you think you've found her?" Harlan asked impatiently.

"I don't know," Betty said. "The people in that part of the country are a little standoffish. They won't talk to a white person at all, claiming they don't *habla ingles*. They won't even talk to Latinos if they don't know them, but I got the feeling this woman on the phone was very nervous and eager to end the conversation. I just had a hunch it might be the woman you're seeking."

"Do you think it would be worth my while to drive over there and check it out?" Harlan asked.

"I can't answer that. I know I don't want to go in there all by my lonesome. It's not that I'm afraid, it's just that my momma didn't raise a fool," Betty advised.

"I'll talk to my boss and see what he recommends." Harlan said, "I'll let you know."

The spring roundup was a little later than normal due to the changing of the guard. All the mama cows and their calves in each section were gathered into whatever working pens were in that area. The only dip tank on the ranch was down the Rayado River a couple of miles from Rayado camp at a very large set of working pens and shipping chutes. At the other pens the cattle had to be sprayed. The routine was for all the cowboys that worked for the ranch, along with quite a few day workers, to gather very early in the morning, usually before sunrise, at a designated place, get their instructions from the ramrod, and fan out to push all the cattle toward the working pens. Ideally when a gather was started the cattle would still be on their bed ground. This was all done horseback, of course.

The cattle, usually between two hundred and four hundred head, were driven into a large pen to be held. If there wasn't a large pen then they were held by several riders, usually kids or less experienced cowboys. Normally there were two teams of flankers, one or two ropers, one brander, one cutter, and one vaccinator. A bunch of calves would be driven into a smaller corral where the branding pot or fire was set up. A few mama cows would be allowed in this group to keep the calves from getting too excited.

A horseback roper would cast his loop, usually catching both hind legs, and drag the calf to the flankers. There is a skill involved in this, bordering on an art form. Normally the most skilled ropers at a gather were selected for this job. When the roper drags the calf to a team of flankers, one of them grabs the tail of the calf and gives a little tug that flips the calf onto its side. He then gets down on the calf, one knee on its neck and one on the shoulders, holding the front legs so they don't thrash about. The other flanker, who sits on the ground, holds onto the top back leg with both hands and hooks his boot heel behind the other one. This prevents the calf from kicking with its powerful hind legs.

While the calf is being held, the cutter descends and, if it's a bull calf, relieves the critter of its family jewels. After he cuts out the testicles, the cutter throws them in a bucket. The vaccinator gives the calf whatever shots are required. The brander grabs a hot branding iron out of the pot or fire and places the brand on the appropriate spot. The flankers have to make sure the correct side is facing up. Two efficient ropers can keep two sets of flankers and everyone else very busy, but one good roper is usually just right.

When this whole scenario is working efficiently it is a thing of beauty. In just a few hours a large herd of calves will all be worked. When the job is finished, all hands will be covered in sweat and dirt, even when the weather is cool. The calves are then herded back to be 'mothered up' with their mamas. Any time there is a situation where calves and cows are separated, such as during a trail drive or a branding, the job is always finished by allowing the mama cows and calves to get 'mothered up' again. Some veteran cow folks, men and women alike, can tell which calf belongs to each cow.

Everyone then heads back to Rayado camp to leave their buckets of "mountain oysters" at the cookhouse to be fried and eater later. This would usually occur when the spring roundup was finished and a cookout would be held for all ranch employees. The next morning the whole process starts again at a different site, and the roundup continues until every unbranded calf on the ranch has been tended to.

A few days after their previous conversation, Harlan got permission from his boss to go to New Mexico and follow up on his leads. He informed Betty and set the time when he planned to arrive. After meeting Betty at her office, they travelled together in her unit. They went first to Moreno Valley, then on toward Ocate, passing Black Lakes. Betty pinpointed exactly where Tony Garcia's ranch was located, and they arrived there in the early afternoon. At first glance it seemed like no one was about. Betty knocked several times on the front door of the house and was about to give up when the door opened a crack and a man's voice said in Spanish,

"What do you want?"

"I'm Deputy Betty Rodriquez from Colfax County," she said, answering in Spanish and showing her shield. "We're looking for Tony Garcia."

"What do you want him for?" the man asked.

"We think he might have had contact with a fugitive from Colorado, and we wanted to ask him some questions concerning that," Betty stated as she was joined by Harlan, who had been looking around the barnyard and corrals for a vehicle, horse trailer, or horse that he might recognize.

The door opened a little further, "What's this person's name you're looking for?" the man asked.

"Nora Lackey from Walsenburg, Colorado," Harlan answered. "May we come in?"

The door opened all the way and a Latino man about fifty years old dressed in jeans, boots, and a western shirt invited them in. He was a handsome man with some gray at the temples, but the rest of his hair was almost black, as were his eyes.

"Come into the kitchen. I was fixing a bite to eat. Can I get you some coffee?"

"Yes, that would be nice," Betty said as she and Harlan settled down at the kitchen table. "Are you Tony Garcia?"

"Yes. I'm sorry for the cool reception. You guys took me by surprise," Tony replied, joining them at the table with coffee pot in hand to make sure his guest's mugs were full.

"We believe Mrs. Lackey was talking to you in a bar in Angel Fire about a week or ten days ago. Is that true?" Harlan asked, showing Tony a picture of Nora Lackey.

"Yes, she came over to the table where I was sitting and struck up a conversation," Tony answered, looking at the picture. "She wanted to know if I had a place to board her horse."

"Did she say where she was from or where she was headed?" Harlan asked.

"She said she was from Colorado and looking for a new place to settle. She needed somewhere to keep her horse until she found a place. What's this all about anyway?"

"Did she come here, and if she did, is she still here?"

"Yeah, she came here for a few days, but left in a hurry yesterday, taking her horse and all her stuff with her. Tell you the truth, I'm kinda glad she's gone. At first it was good—you know it gets kinda lonely out here all by myself. The sex was good, but then she started to talk about how her husband had been murdered and how the mur-

183

derers were looking for her, and she wanted to know if I'd protect her. I drew the line at that and was wondering what I'd got myself into. What's she done?" Tony asked.

"She is wanted on suspicion of murder in Huerfano County, Colorado. Is it all right if we look around to make sure she has gone?" Harlan asked.

"Murder!" Tony said shocked, "Look around all you want. I'm telling you she left yesterday about mid-afternoon."

"Did she say where she was going?" Betty asked.

"No, and I never asked. Actually I was glad to see her dust. I can't see the entrance to my lane from here, so I don't know which way she turned when she got to the main road," Tony answered.

Betty looked around in the house and Harlan checked the outbuildings, but there was no one else on the property. They thanked Tony for his cooperation and getting into Betty's unit left the premises. When they got to the main road Betty asked,

"Which way—right or left?"

"I don't think she went back toward Angel Fire, do you? I bet she went to Wagon Mound and got on the Interstate," Harlan mused.

"You think she is headed south, then?" Betty asked.

"It's a lot easier to hide yourself in a bigger city like Santa Fe or Albuquerque than in these small communities. Have we got an APB out on her?"

"Yes, we do. The state police will probably see her if she

is on the highway," Betty answered.

Betty and Harlan showed the picture of the fugitive at the convenience stores and gas stations around Wagon Mound without success. Also, no one had seen a pickup pulling a horse trailer that matched the description, so they assumed the fugitive had continued south on I-25.

"Do you have in your case files the kind of credit card she is using? If she is still using it, we might be able to tell where she is going," Betty stated.

"Good idea," Harlan said, calling his office in Walsenburg via the unit's radio.

It was getting late so they decided to return to Cimarron. On the way back Harlan received a call from his boss asking him to return to Colorado. Apparently the Huerfano County law enforcement leaders, the sheriff and the DA, decided they could depend on New Mexico lawmen to find and arrest Nora Lackey. Harlan thanked Betty and her team for all their help and headed home.

A short while after the spring branding was completed the cattle were pushed to certain pastures that had access to high mountain country. There were several high country areas on the ranch where mesa tops ranged between seven and eight thousand feet in elevation, along with one pasture containing more than twenty-thousand acres that ran up to ten thousand feet or more in altitude. Many of the older cows knew the trails to these high country pastures and would start up on their own, taking their calves with them. A few cows had to be driven up the cattle drives.

About three hundred replacement heifers were put on top of one mesa that had approximately five thousand acres of excellent grass. There was only one trail to the top of this mesa, and getting that many young "girls" up that trail was a challenge. The easiest way was to put one old mama cow in the bunch and let her lead the way, with all the young debutantes following her. There were windmills on top of that mesa, so the heifers had plenty of water and grass for the summer and were safe from amorous bulls.

The heifers were not bred until they were old enough to

have babies safely. The job for the cowboys at the different camps was to keep an eye on the cattle in the high country. This required riding through the grazing herds every couple of days to make sure the mamas and the babies were doing all right.

Betty thought it was strange that the state police had not contacted her to report sighting the vehicle that Nora Lackey was driving. She concluded that maybe the fugitive had not taken the interstate highway, but possibly took back roads when she left Ocate. Coincidentally about this time Tomas Torrez, a deputy for Mora County, was driving his unit into Mora and was in the left-turn lane waiting for traffic to pass so he could pull into the parking lot of the courthouse. He had just heard the APB on the radio a few minutes before, when coincidently a faded blue Ford pickup pulling a gray horse trailer passed him in the oncoming lane. The vehicle was driven by a woman.

Instead of pulling into the parking lot, the deputy made a U-turn and began following the pickup and trailer, allowing an interval of several car-lengths. Tomas was a ten year veteran of the Mora County Sheriff's Department. He was about five foot six inches tall and built like a refrigerator. He had dark hair and eyes, and was usually considered mild-mannered and thoughtful unless he was riled.

When he had verified the license plate number on the horse trailer, he relayed the information to his dispatcher and suggested they notify the sheriff's department in Colfax County. He also asked for guidance as to whether he should stop the vehicle or just follow it. The response was to attempt to stop the vehicle, but to be alert because the woman was considered armed and dangerous. He followed the vehicle going west on the highway leading to Penasco for several miles. About a half mile further on he knew there was a wide spot on the right shoulder of the highway so he flipped on his lights and siren. As he expected the truck pulled off the highway and stopped.

After radioing the dispatcher he left his unit and proceeded on foot toward the stopped pickup, making sure his weapon was readily available. Tomas stayed close to the bed of the pickup as he approached the driver's door, his dark eyes darting from the driver to her hands.

"Why are you stopping me? I haven't done anything wrong," the woman driver asked scornfully.

"Keep both hands where I can see them, please, ma'am," Tomas requested.

"This is ridiculous. I'm in a hurry. How long is this going to take?"

"The brake lights on your horse trailer are not working properly. Would you let me see your driver's license please," Tomas answered, watching carefully as the woman's hands moved from the door to the seat on her right.

When the hands came back up toward the open window, one of them had a pistol in it. Tomas instinctively moved closer to the bed of the pickup and was reaching for his own weapon when her gun went off, firing into the ground beside the pickup. At the same time the vehicle was placed in gear and, with tires spinning and gravel flying, the pickup sped off. Tomas had to jump clear to keep from being hit by the horse trailer.

Running back to his unit he radioed the dispatcher to report what had happened and began pursuing the speeding pickup and trailer. He kept his lights and siren on, but stayed back a few car-lengths from the fugitive. There wasn't enough time to set up a roadblock before they reached Penasco, but to Tomas's surprise the vehicle turned right on the high road to Taos. He had assumed the fugitive would continue west toward the main highway between Taos and Santa Fe.

Tomas stayed back at a safe distance and made radio contact with the Taos County Sheriff, asking them to set up a roadblock where the high road intersected the main highway at Rancho de Taos. The road they were on was a narrow mountain track with lots of twists and turns. Staying about a half mile behind the fleeing vehicle, Tomas observed the pickup pulling off the road at the top of the pass onto a US Forest Service road. He continued past this turn-off, hoping the woman would think he missed her turn.

Turning off his lights and siren, he made a U-turn, keeping everyone informed by radio of the situation. He decided to follow cautiously, so he turned onto the Forest Service road. This path was very rough and he had to go slowly to keep the unit from high-centering. There was a lot of timber and brush at this altitude in the mountains, so the visibility was not very clear. Tomas followed the road for approximately a mile when he came to a little clearing. The pickup and horse trailer were parked at a gate in a fence line. The rear gate of the horse trailer was standing open and the horse was gone. Tomas placed a call on his radio and left his vehicle very cautiously, with weapon drawn as he approached the pickup. The cab of the truck was empty and the woman was nowhere to be seen. He walked to the gate in the fence, which it had been opened and thrown back. There were horse tracks on the ground indicating the horse had gone through the gate.

Doug was riding Pingo early one morning, intent on checking the grass conditions on top of Ortega Mesa. Dub wanted to put two or three dozen mares with colts on the mesa for the summer, figuring that after a summer up there in that rock pile the colts would become very adept at getting around in the rocks. The mesa was somewhat level on top with a couple of canyons bisecting it. It was very rocky and high enough in elevation to have a few aspen groves.

The grass was usually good despite the rocky conditions. One stud named Colonel would be placed with the mares to offer protection and to get the next generation started. Some of the hands called him "The Colonel," and he was a beautiful quarter horse stud, grulla in color, with a dark gray mane and tail. The Colonel had produced some excellent colts and was a good choice to put with the mares. He was getting on in years but could still do the job. That evening Doug trimmed his hooves, with the help of Hugh, in a corral at Rayado camp where the Colonel spent the winters.

Hugh was supposed to hold the lead rope taut while Doug worked on the horse's feet. Hugh became a little lackadaisical and allowed too much slack on the lead rope, so while Doug was trimming a front foot, the Colonel reached around and grabbed a chunk of Doug's ass in his teeth—not hard, because if he wanted to he could have taken out a piece of meat. It was just enough to let Doug know he was getting close to the quick. Stallions have very powerful jaws and can do some serious damage if they are so inclined. Doug rose up cussing Hugh for not holding the horse's head. Hugh started sputtering and spitting tobacco juice on everything in the vicinity.

The next morning Doug was riding up the trail that went to the top of Ortega Mesa, commonly referred to as the Goat camp trail. He passed an area that was sub-irrigated from a seep spring near the base of the mesa bluff. There was about an acre of green grass at this spot and a mama cow was getting her belly full on the delicacy. Nearby her calf was running and playing in the sunshine. Doug stopped his horse to let him blow, also allowing time to take in the pastoral scene.

As his eyes were scanning the landscape, he noticed a movement from the top of a huge rock that had rolled off the bluff eons ago. There was a big mountain lion bunching himself and preparing to leap onto the baby calf. In an instant Doug whipped out his 30-30 carbine and fired just as the cat leaped. The bullet ricocheted off the rock but startled the cat enough to cause him to miss the calf. BC had seen the cat at the same instant and was bounding to the rescue. He had a bit of a tussle with the big cat, who was soon running and leaping up the rocky bluff. The baby calf ran to his mother and was hiding under her belly, peeking out as if to say, "Hey, guys, what's going on?" BC came trotting back to Doug with that look on his face again: "Well, I saved your ass again, Mr. Sharpshooter."

"Yeah, I know. What would I ever do without you," Doug mumbled.

Betty was in her office studying maps trying to figure out where the fugitive might be headed. Deputies from Mora and Taos counties had completed forensics on the vehicle left behind by the woman, and they moved them to an impound yard in Taos. A Taos County Sheriff's posse composed of volunteers had followed the tracks for several miles, but they gave up the search when it became evident that the horse had passed into Colfax County. The rider evidently had fencing pliers with her, for whenever she encountered a fence she would cut the wires.

Betty called Harlan to give him a heads-up on what was happening.

"I think she is heading back into Colfax County, but I can't figure out where she's going. According to her general line of travel, she is heading for Black Lakes or maybe back to Angel Fire. If I can get permission from my boss, I'm going back up there to get it sorted out," Betty explained.

"If you need me to come back over there, please let me know. I'll see if I can get permission. My boss is worried about money as usual, budget cuts and all," Harlan answered.

The next morning Betty went to Moreno Valley to show the photo of Nora Lackey. She finally hit pay dirt at the convenience store located outside of Angel Fire. The clerk remembered that the woman came in the previous morning. She purchased some groceries, a bottle of whiskey, and several bottles of water. The clerk had assumed the woman arrived by car, but after the woman left the store she rode away on a horse, with her purchases tied on the back of the saddle. The clerk hadn't noticed which way the woman was going, as the store was busy at the time. After spending the rest of the day trying to find someone else who had seen the fugitive, Betty finally returned to Cimarron.

Doug, John, and Fro met at Rayado camp early one morning, at first light of course, and proceeded to push some cows, assisted by their dogs, through the gate going into Mora Creek pasture. The three men spread out, intent on herding all the cows that were in this pasture up toward the cattle drive. Doug took the left flank, Fro the right, and John the middle. There were a lot of pinon, cedar, and juniper in this pasture, so it took considerable zig-zagging to make sure they got all the cattle moving in the right direction.

Doug was riding in the shadow of the bluffs of Ortega Mesa and crossed several small canyons running down from the mesa. He rode across the mouth of Mora Creek Canyon or Diablo Canyon, as some people called it. It was an extremely rough and treacherous canyon, and a hell of a place to lose a cow. Doug saw some magpies fly up from a short distance into the canyon, and some ravens were gathered at the same place. He cautiously rode toward this spot with his hand resting on the stock of his carbine.

About a hundred yards up, Dunny snorted and started walking stiff-legged. BC proceeded toward the site growling and with hackles raised. Doug dismounted and tied Dunny securely to a nearby pinon tree. With carbine in hand, he walked cautiously to the kill site, for a cow and her calf had both been killed and were lying about fifty yards apart. BC already determined that it was a bear, but not a grizzly this time. Probably a very large member of the black bear species, "Though not exactly black," Doug mused after finding some hair on a tree the bear had brushed past. "This looks red to me," he muttered as he held the few hairs up to the morning light. He put the hair in his shirt pocket, then made sure the cow had been killed by a bear—checking its nose and looking to see if the neck was broken. He went to retrieve his horse, who was still nervous and rolling his eyes.

"It's me, Dunny. No need to get silly," Doug reassured the horse. Calling BC he started back toward the herd, meeting John about halfway there.

"Come to check on you," John yelled, "What's with those birds up there?"

"Bear killed a cow and a calf. Looks like a red colored bear," Doug answered, riding up to John and showing him the strands of hair.

"I'll be damned. I've heard talk that there is a big red bear living in this canyon, but nothing about it being a cow killer," John said.

"Looks like we have a cow-killing bear and possibly a calf-killing mountain lion in the area," Doug offered. "I'll let Dub know when I get back to camp."

By the time they pushed all the cattle up the cattle drive and waited for them to mother up when they got on top, it was getting late. It was essential for the mamas and babies to find each other, otherwise a mama would go back to the last place she had seen her calf to hunt for it. Some calves would keep up with their mamas on a drive, but most would bunch up at the rear of the herd and be lost to their mamas until they found each other at the end of the drive.

When the riders got back to their vehicles and horse trailers and returned to their respective camps, it was getting on to dark-thirty. As is often the case with ranch life, chores were done by lantern light. Doug called the ramrod, Dub, and informed him about the dead cow and calf, and that predators were out and about. If he wanted to hire a professional hunter to take care of business, Doug recommended Bobby Daugherty. He was sure Bobby wouldn't mind traveling over Raton Pass, especially for a paid hunt. Since it wasn't hunting season yet for either bear or mountain lion, Dub doubted if the wildlife department would give permission to take either animal. Maybe a wait-and-see approach would be the best way to handle the problem for now. In the meantime all hands should keep a sharp lookout for depredations and ride through the cattle as often as possible.

It wasn't necessary to tell Doug this, for he planned on being back on top with the cattle in the summer pasture the next day. Now that he was a married man, he liked this new arrangement, which meant that he didn't have to stay at a remote cow camp all summer. It required a lot more riding, but on the plus side he was home every night with his lovely bride. Staying in a high country cow camp for the summer was fun for a while when he was young and single, but now he had responsibilities.

The ranch owned several pieces of heavy equipment, and they hired operators to carve out a road to the high country. When finished this would allow trucks and vehicles pulling horse trailers to have full access to that part of the ranch. There were several high mountain lakes full of trout in this area, so it opened the possibility of letting people in who were willing to pay for the privilege of fishing there.

This particular high country pasture was about twenty thousand acres in size, divided between spruce, fir, aspen, and pine forest, as well as large open grassy parks that were ablaze with wildflowers in the spring. After riding for several hours, Doug finally broke out of the timber onto the edge of a huge meadow that was called Aqua Fria Park. A couple of miles out in the middle of the park, Aqua Fria Lake glistened like a gem. This was a lake that had about twenty surface acres. Doug pulled out his binoculars, thinking his eyes had deceived him, for he thought he glimpsed a wisp of smoke on the other side of the park.

Garcia cow camp, or the remnants of that cow camp, was

about four miles away on the far side of the park. Years ago it had been an active cow camp in the summer, but the only thing left now was the log cabin and a small corral behind it. Doug glassed the cabin and surrounding area thoroughly, satisfying himself that he had indeed seen smoke coming out of the chimney. He decided to stay at the edge of the park in the timber and try to get closer to the cabin.

After riding about three more miles, he was within a couple of miles, so he once again studied the cabin through the binoculars. From this vantage point he could see a horse in the corral. "Hmm, I think I know that horse," he mused. Even at this distance he was fairly sure it was Lackey's horse.

"I don't think I want to approach that woman by myself way out here. I've seen what she can do," he told BC, who readily agreed with him.

Doug rode another two or three miles to the western edge of the property which was marked by a fence line. He found the gate in this fence to make sure it was closed, as there were cattle in this pasture now. He also noticed that someone had recently brought a horse through the gate, and he was sure it was the same horse he had seen before in the corral at Garcia cow camp. If one went through the gate and down the mountain on the west side of the fence, he would end up in Angel Fire. Since Doug had been isolated in the backcountry, he didn't yet know about the pursuit of Nora Lackey.

He decided he'd better head for home because it was at least twenty miles away, and he wanted to check on the cows along the way. When he arrived at the top of the cattle drive he noticed that the road construction crew had gotten as far as the gate at the head of that trail. He decided to take this new road down the bluff. Although far from being finished, it was still better than going down the rugged cattle drive. The new road had lots of hairpin curves, but Doug figured he could get a pickup and trailer over it in a few days. When he got home and finished the chores it was late, so he called Harlan at home.

"Hey, sweetheart, how's it going?" Doug asked when Celeste answered the phone.

"We are all fine here. How are you guys?" Celeste asked. "How are Rita and the baby?"

"Rita's getting big—looks like it's going to be a healthy sized baby. You can talk to her in a minute, but I need to bend Harlan's ear for a second. Is he there?" Doug asked.

"Hey, cowboy," Harlan said when he got on the line. "What's up?"

"I know where your fugitive is. There is a cabin up in the high country on this ranch, and I saw smoke coming out of the chimney and her horse in the corral there today," Doug explained.

"You're kidding me. The law in New Mexico has been chasing her all over the northern part of the state. Did she see you?" Harlan asked.

"No, I made sure she didn't. Since there is no one up there, she probably feels safe for a while. Let me know what you decide to do. If you need to come here, I've got a horse for you to ride and you can stay at our house. Bring Celeste and the kids. They would love it here," Doug said.

"Thanks, we just might do that. Celeste is here and wants to talk to Rita. I'll let you know what's been decided," Harlan said handing the phone to Celeste.

Harlan had some vacation time coming, so with permission from his boss, he loaded up the family and headed to New Mexico. School was out for the summer, and they had plenty of time for a trip. When they arrived at Rita and Doug's house everyone got reacquainted, and the kids ran around checking out all the new sights—especially the horses. Doug saddled a couple of the gentler mares and the kids rode around the yard until dark. Harlan called Betty since they were in her jurisdiction, and she agreed to join them at the ranch the next morning.

Their horses were saddled by first light and they had time for a second cup of coffee before Betty arrived. They loaded the horses in a trailer, because Doug was purty sure he could get a pickup truck and trailer close to the edge of Agua Fria Park. When they got to the point where the road crew cut the road up through the rim rock it was slow going and Doug had to downshift into granny gear, but they kept going until they reached La Grulla camp. It was located in the first big park in this section of the high country. Here they unloaded the horses and went the rest of the way on horseback.

As they neared the larger Agua Fria Park they dismounted and stayed in the trees to avoid detection. From there they could use binoculars to observe the cabin which sat about three or four miles across the park. There was a horse grazing in front of the cabin, but no other sign of activity. They remounted and, staying out of sight of anyone who might be in the cabin, they took a winding route that came in behind the corral. They left their horses tied in the trees to prevent them from nickering to the horse at the cabin.

All three crept up from behind the cabin, with Harlan and Betty easing around to the front. It was difficult to see inside, since most of the windows were boarded up. A thin tendril of smoke was coming from the chimney. Letting Betty know by hand signals what he intended to do, Harlan drew his weapon and opened the front door to rush inside.

There was no need for apprehension, though, because Nora Lackey was not going to be a threat to anyone ever again. She was lying in a pool of blood on the floor with a black hole in her forehead.

"What the hell is going on?" Harlan declared in disgust.

Doug came rushing around the cabin and into the front door. He took one look and was sickened at the sight before him. Betty sat down in the rickety chair, looking pale and making the sign of the cross.

"May God have mercy," she said. "I don't think this was suicide, do you Harlan?"

Harlan was looking at the tracks in the dust on the floor.

"Don't anyone walk around too much. We need to preserve what forensic evidence we have. There is a track here that doesn't match any of our footprints or hers. It looks like it was made by a hiking boot."

Betty and Doug went outside, and Betty got on her handheld radio. She tried to call the sheriff's department, but there was no signal. They looked around for tracks or any other evidence that might be visible. Doug went behind the cabin to the corral to see if there were any other tracks. All three of them eventually gathered in front of the cabin.

"There isn't much more we can do here. Let's go back and call your office, Betty," Harlan suggested.

They secured the cabin with police tape, and propped up the door as best as they could.

"Whoever came in here knew she was here. I've got a theory. I think when she went to that convenience store in Angel Fire about a week ago she called someone. There is a pay phone there and I bet if we do a search of the calls made from that pay phone we can find out who she called. Is there access to this place from that side of the mountain?" Betty asked Doug.

"Yes, about a mile west of where our horses are tied is a fence line that runs north and south. There is a gate in that fence and a road comes up from the west side. The entrance to that road is down in the valley almost within the town limits of Angel Fire," Doug answered.

"Let's ride over to that gate and see if there are any tracks. Keep your eyes peeled for anything between here and there," Harlan ordered.

When they arrived at the gate they tied their horses and began investigating the area. They found where a vehicle with Jeep-type tire treads had parked and turned around. Harlan covered up a portion of those tracks with tree limbs and rocks in order to preserve them. They also found a footprint made by a hiking boot with a waffle pattern, so he preserved it in the same manner.

Betty checked her radio again and discovered it had a signal. She radioed her headquarters and informed them of what they had found. Her boss, the Colfax County sheriff, said he would dispatch a forensic team and the coroner as soon as possible. This team would meet with Betty at her office in Cimarron, probably the next morning. The three of them returned to Doug's pickup by the most direct route, arriving at Rayado camp very late.

The next morning Betty met the forensic team, a couple of deputies, and the coroner at her office in Cimarron. They all proceeded caravan-style to Angel Fire. When she got to the convenience store where she assumed Nora Lackey may have made a phone call, she stopped and recorded the phone number. They continued up the rugged canyon road after radioing the dispatcher to get the phone records for that number.

Betty stopped at the gate, which provided access to the road leading to Garcia camp. As she let all the vehicles through and closed the gate, she noticed a yellow neck scarf tied to the gate post. They proceeded to the last gate at the top of the ridge, which was about six miles further up the canyon. After getting plaster casts of the tire marks and footprints, they continued to the cabin where the coroner and the forensic team went through their thorough routine. The coroner finished his examination first and enlisted help to load the body into his station wagon. It took another hour for the forensic people to finish their work, and the whole caravan left the mountain by the same way they had come.

After Doug had explained to Rita what they found, she declared,

"It's a shame that lady's life was so screwed up, that this is how she left this world. Sometimes people make very self-destructive choices," she continued.

"I guess we'll never know the answer to that one," Doug offered. "I've wondered why bad things happen to good people, not that she was a good or bad person. Sometimes it's because of bad choices, but sometimes it's just being in the wrong place at the wrong time."

"Yeah, I know what you mean. I've often wondered about that, too."

"I was at my dad's funeral and a preacher told me afterward that it was God's will. My answer to him was, "Bullshit. God don't kill people." The preacher was quite taken aback, but I firmly believe that. Dying is just part of nature. A plant lives and flourishes, produces something, then dies. Animals do the same, and so do humans. What's important to God is how a man lives his life while he's here. That woman that died up there at the cow camp knew something about somebody that scared the hell out of that person—so much so that they had to make sure she never told anyone whatever it was she knew. It seems convoluted, but it's simple really," Doug said.

"All Harlan has to do is figure out who that somebody is," Rita added.

Harlan was thinking the same thing after he returned to his office in La Veta. He had just received a call from Betty Rodriquez, and the results of the phone record search from the convenience store listed only one call that could have been made by Nora Lackey. It was to the bar where she had worked for many years in Walsenburg. "Whoever answered that call has some explaining to do," Harlan mused.

The next morning he and Sheriff Sisneros went to that bar and found the place empty, except for the owner who was also the day bartender. Jerry Whitford was a big guy, thick through the chest, big arms and legs, and a good sized pot-gut hanging over his belt. He had a bald bullet-like head and tattoos on the side of his neck and on both arms.

"Mr. Whitford," Harlan said, showing his shield, "I am Harlan Martinez and this is Sheriff Sisneros. Do you mind answering a few questions?"

"Most folks call me Bruiser. What's this about?" The barkeep replied.

"There was a telephone call placed to your phone a week ago about 5:00 PM from Nora Lackey. Did you take that call?" Harlan asked.

"From Nora! That bitch left me hanging. She was supposed to be here working about a month ago, but never showed up and I haven't seen her since. The only phone in this place is that pay phone," he said nodding toward the wall near the end of the bar. "Anybody could have answered that phone. When we're busy I don't answer it because one of the customers or waitresses will get it eventually," he added.

Harlan went over to the pay phone and jotted down the number.

"Do you know who could have answered it at 5:00 PM one week ago today?" Sheriff Sisneros asked.

"No, we get pretty busy usually every day about that time," Bruiser answered.

"Do you remember who was in here at that time, and can you tell me if you had any waitresses working then?" the sheriff asked.

"You're talking about a week ago—I can't remember who was in here yesterday," Bruiser answered roughly.

"We can do this the easy way or the hard way," the sheriff stated very firmly, looking Bruiser straight in the eye. "We can move this interview to my office, and I'll have my forensic people go over this place with a fine-tooth comb. We could subpoena your personnel records, which could take about a month or two, during which time you will be shut down."

Bruiser blanched, chuckling nervously, "You wouldn't do that would you?"

"Try me," the sheriff answered firmly. Bruiser looked for help from Harlan who was smiling and nodding.

"Okay, I'll cooperate. What do you want to know?" Bruiser asked sheepishly.

"Who answered the phone when Nora called? If not you, who?" the sheriff persisted.

"It was probably Candice. She was working as a waitress then, but there were a bunch of bikers in here and its possible one of them answered it," he stated.

"Names," the sheriff demanded.

Harlan wrote the names in his notebook as Bruiser spat them out. He also took down the phone number and address of the waitress Candice Velez.

"Did any of the people that were in here at the time mention that Nora had called? If someone else answered the phone, did they tell you about it?" Harlan asked.

Bruiser blanched again and swallowed hard, after thinking about it for a while he said, "Yeah, Candice mentioned that Nora had called and apologized for not coming to work, but I never talked to her."

"You could have told us that up front, and it would have made this a whole lot easier," the sheriff added. "Did she talk to anyone else other than Candice?"

"Yeah, I'm purty sure she talked to Spider, but I don't know how for long."

"Who is Spider?" Harlan asked.

"He is a biker who comes in here once in a while. I don't know what his real name is or where he is from," Bruiser explained.

"If he ever comes back in here again, call me immediately," Harlan stated, handing Bruiser one of his business cards.

Doug was remiss in his duties of checking on the mama cows and their babies, so the next morning after Celeste and Harlan left he saddled up and was out among the cattle. He rode through bunches of grazing cattle looking for any problems. In the afternoon he noticed a cow that had a tight bag and one of the teats had a wound. The cow's calf was following the mama around, bawling with hunger. It was obvious that this cow had an injury and was sore, because every time the calf tried to suck the cow would kick him off.

Doug decided he should try to rope the cow and doctor her here, since he was some distance from a pen or corral. Roping her was easy, but trying to get her throwed was another story. Fortunately he was riding Frog Honey who was a very smart cow pony. Frog kept the rope tight while Doug, on foot, grabbed the cow's tail and attempted to pull her over to her side. After several attempts and getting kicked a couple of times he finally succeeded.

While getting her legs tied with his piggin' string he got popped by one of her hind feet, and he took the blow on his left leg above the knee. The pain was excruciating for a bit, but he finally got all the cow's legs tied securely. He retrieved a can of Bag Balm from his saddlebag and massaged it into the cow's udder, milking her enough to relieve the tight bag. He had some wound medicine that would help heal the sore and keep off the flies. It tasted so bad that the calf would probably not suck on that teat.

Having done all he could do for this mama, he first untied the lariat around the head then untied the piggin' string that was holding the feet. The mama cow thanked him by regaining her feet and charging him. Doug wasn't in the mood to play games so he swatted her in the face with his hat and told her to go find her baby, while he limped lamely back to his horse.

The next day Harlan located where Candice lived and called on her.

"Good morning, I'm Harlan Martinez of the Huerfano County Sheriff's Office. Are you Candice Velez?" he asked.

"Yes, I am. What's this about?" she asked with a note of concern in her voice.

"We are investigating the death of Nora Lackey and we have reason to believe that you were one of the last people to talk to her," Harlan said.

"Nora is dead?" Candice asked, visible shaken. "You better come in."

Once they were seated in Candice's living room Harlan continued,

"Nora called the bar where you work about a week ago, and you answered the phone and talked to her. We want to know what was said in that conversation."

"How did she die? She sounded okay on the phone. She said she was in New Mexico. What on earth happened?" Candice asked.

"Did she say where she was exactly?" Harlan asked.

"No, she said she was calling from a pay phone and that she was somewhere in New Mexico. I asked her when she was coming back, that Bruiser was really pissed, and that I had to work both her shift and mine. I was being yelled at by someone who wanted another round, so I handed the phone to Spider," Candice explained.

"You just happened to hand the phone to Spider?" Harlan asked.

"No, when he realized who I was talking to he wanted to talk to her. He and his buddies were sitting at the table close to the phone."

"Then what happened?"

"I took care of several customers. We were very busy and I was the only waitress."

"Did you talk to Nora again?"

"No. When I glanced over I noticed that Spider had hung up the phone."

"Were you and Nora very close?"

"Yeah, I suppose so. We worked together for nearly ten years. We talked a lot and got to know each other pretty well."

"Did you know why she was running from the law?" Harlan asked.

"I think some of the things Nora told me were secrets, and I don't think she would want me to tell anyone," Candice said.

"This is a murder investigation, so its very important that we know all the facts. It would be best if you told us everything you know," Harlan advised.

"So you're saying Nora was murdered?"

"Yes, she was."

"Oh my God!" Candice said crying.

"We need to know what was happening in Nora's life, and maybe you can help us with that," Harlan offered.

"Like what?" Candice asked, recovering a little from the shock.

"Like why she killed Angela Ransom. What caused her to do such an irrational thing as that?"

Candice sat quietly looking at her hands for some time before she raised her eyes wet with tears and looked at Harlan.

"She had problems. She was very emotional and paranoid about her husband cheating on her. I think she was a very jealous person who let her jealousy eat at her too much. She always said that if she could find the woman her husband was having an affair with, she would kill her. I tried to convince her that he wasn't worth it. I had met him and I didn't think he was anything special. I think he was one of those men who come on to all women, but I found him disgusting."

"She had convinced herself the affair was with a women who worked at the library in La Veta. I guess this was because when they had a fight, which was often, they would shout things at each other that they knew would hurt. I figured he must have said something to her that made her think the women in La Veta was the one. After his death she read the articles in the paper about his murder and your investigation, and she came to the conclusion that the woman named Angela was her husband's lover and also his killer. She was obsessed with that."

"Did she tell you that she had killed Angela?" Harlan asked.

"No, I never saw her again after that. She left this part of the country, and I didn't know where she went," Candice answered.

"Did she know this biker called Spider whom she talked to on the phone?"

"Yes, she knew him. He and his friends were in here often, and I think she and Spider had gone to a motel a few times in the past."

"So she didn't want her husband to have an affair, but it was all right if she did."

"Her husband was dead," Candice said defensively.

"We have evidence that she was having affairs before his death."

"She was a good-looking woman. Men found her attractive, she loved to be adored, and besides she was...I think they call it narcissistic."

"Do you have any idea why she decided to hide out in a cabin in the mountains of New Mexico?" Harlan asked.

"She told me one time that her father had been a cowboy and had worked on several ranches in Colorado and New Mexico. She said once that the family had spent part of a summer at a cow camp in New Mexico when she was a little girl, and that it was one of the best memories she had of her childhood."

"Do you know where we can find Spider?"

"You don't think he could have killed her, do you?" Candice asked.

"We need to talk to him. Do you know where he lives?"

"I think he lives in Trinidad, but I'm not sure about that."

Doug was riding in the high country pasture when he noticed some cow and calf tracks being followed by shod horse tracks. He began trailing the tracks, puzzling over what this could mean. It was either someone rustling cattle or a cowboy from a neighboring ranch bringing home some strays. He followed the tracks until they came to a gate that was in the property line fence with the Mora Ranch. Whoever had driven the cows with calves had closed the gate behind him.

Doug did likewise, following the tracks on the neighbor's ranch for several miles and finally coming to a watering hole where two cows and their calves stood resting. The cattle bore the brand of the Mora Ranch. Evidently one of their cowboys noticed some missing cattle and found them on the XL Bar, so he drove them back to where they belonged.

By this time Doug was far south of where he normally

dropped off the mesa so he decided to ride east, crossing back over onto XL Bar property and dropping down the mountain above Abreu camp, where John and Sonja and their family lived. This was all new country to him, as he had not seen it before, and he came off the mesa on a narrow twisting trail that had a fence with a gate at the bottom where the trail leveled out. He went through this gate, closing it, and proceeded across a corner of a pasture that was between two mesas, heading toward another gate on a trail that led to Abreu camp.

Suddenly he noticed a band of mares with one of the ranch's studs named Prince about four hundred yards to the south. Doug was riding Big Red, a proud cut gelding, which means he had all the attributes of a stud but could not pass them on to his progeny. Prince saw Doug at the same time, and he came running with ears laid back, teeth bared, head low to the ground, and screaming at every breath. Doug spurred Big Red and they took off as fast as they could go.

When about two hundred yards from the gate, it was obvious they were not going to make it, so Doug took down his rope and doubled it to make a whip. He also guided Big Red toward the canyon rim that sloped off about one hundred feet to the bottom and was covered with oak brush. He figured any injuries they might receive from the oaks would be minor compared to a stud getting ahold of them.

As Prince came within biting distance of Big Red, Doug swatted him across the nose with the doubled up rope. This must have hurt because the stud back off for a second, and it gave Big Red time to reach the edge of the canyon. He never slowed down but went sailing off the bluff landing in the oak brush about thirty feet below. The stud gave up the chase, evidently feeling secure that his mares were safe. Big Red went down through the oaks for a ways, finally straddling a tree about three inches in diameter and thirty feet high. It was bent over and pushing up between the horses' front legs. Doug had lost his seat when they first landed in the trees. He got to his feet, found his hat, and discovering his injuries were not too bad, he made his way downhill through the thicket to Big Red. He was finally able to get the big horse off of the tree and they worked their way down through the brush, coming out beside a beautiful stream at the canyon bottom.

Here Doug took off his wild rag and washed their wounds. He decided they were in good enough shape to continue, so they rode up to Abreu camp. There didn't seem to be anyone around, not even the cow dogs. Sonja was probably in the house but didn't come out. John was most likely out checking cows. Doug rode to the saddle barn and found a bottle of medicine that was good for small cuts and abrasions. This he applied liberally on the horse's wounds and then on his. They headed off toward their home camp, but when they were near the intersection of the trail that led up to Rayado Mesa Doug heard someone yell. Soon John rode into view.

"What you doin' way over here? Kinda outta your area aren't you?" John asked while the cow dogs got reacquainted.

"Followed the tracks of someone driving two pair off the ranch. Thought I would investigate, but it turns out they were Mora cattle. By then I was way over there," waving his hand toward the southwest. "Came over the mesa up there and had to fight off Prince. You didn't tell me you had him and a band of mares in that Rock House pasture," Doug answered.

"Geez, you both look like you've been in a fight with a pissed-off bobcat. Did Prince get ahold of you?"

"No but he ran us off that bluff that's above the canyon.

We went down through the oak brush."

"Nah, no one can go down through there with a horse."

"You can if you fly over most of it. Besides I wanted to see you—thought I might catch you laying up there with the dry cows," Doug laughed.

"That'll be the day. I was back there checking on the heifers," John said jerking his thumb toward the mesa that he had just come from. "Rode all the way to the southeast corner where you can look down on the old Martinez Mansion. Old place looks a lot like it used to. Hugh told me all about it."

"When he first started cowboying he rode in there one day—this had to be over seventy years ago. He said he went to the back of the house where the kitchen was, and one of the girls who worked in the kitchen took him to the cellar where they had water running through some troughs with milk and whatever they wanted to keep cool. He said the girl gave him a glass of buttermilk and asked if he wanted some supper."

"The meal wasn't quite ready yet, so the girl took him up to the formal dining room to see how the aristocrats lived. He said everything in the dining room was very ornate with fancy chandeliers and china dishes on the table. He was most astounded by the fact that at each place setting was a large silver ring that had no other purpose than to put a napkin through. Anyway, no one's lived there in over fifty years, but it must have been quite a ranchero in its day. It was part of a Spanish land grant at one time—evidently the heirs sold it off."

This sure was unique country, with places like that dotting the landscape—each with their own special story. John and Doug rode on down the canyon together for a while, talking about the cattle and the land, which were their favorite subjects.

Harlan asked around Walsenburg trying to find out if anyone knew a biker with the nickname of Spider, but he came up empty. He then called his buddy, Deputy Frank Lucero, in Trinidad to see if he knew of anyone by that name.

"Of course I do, and so do you. He's the oldest brother of the Trujillo family. His biker gang mates call him Spider," Frank said.

"I never knew that was what they called him," Harlan exclaimed. "He is back as a person of interest in my murder investigation."

"I thought you had solved that case," Frank stated.

"I thought it was solved too, but then the woman who was involved in the first murder was killed by the victim's wife, who then led us on a long chase across state lines. About two weeks ago we finally traced her to a remote mountain cow camp, only to find that she had been murdered there. Further investigation implicates

Spider," Harlan explained.

"The Trujillos have been fairly quiet lately, ever since that Raton trial, at least here in Trinidad," Frank said.

"I'd really like to talk to him. Would you ask him to come to your office?" Harlan requested.

"I can ask, but that don't mean he'll come in," Frank answered.

Doug returned home late one afternoon, did chores, and went to the house to find Rita in an agitated state.

"What's wrong," he asked, noticing she was obviously upset.

"There is something weird going on in this house," she answered.

"What do you mean, weird?"

"Today I finally had time to get those upstairs bedrooms cleaned and organized. I rearranged furniture, swept and dusted and even moved some pictures on the walls. When I came back down to the kitchen and was fixing supper it sounded like someone was moving furniture upstairs. I first thought it was you trying to play a trick on me, so I rushed upstairs but there was no one there. The furniture was all moved back to where it had been before I moved it. Even the pictures were back to where they had been."

"I looked everywhere upstairs but there was no one else up there. I hollered at whoever it was that was trying to play a trick on me to show themselves but no one answered. It freaked me out, so I came down here and found your old pistol and laid it on the kitchen table there," she nodded toward the old forty-five revolver on the table.

"I'm lucky I didn't get shot when I came in the door," Doug exclaimed.

"The jury's still out on that. You find out who is playing a trick on me or I may start shooting at whoever gets in my sights," Rita said glaring with her hands on her hips.

Doug went upstairs and checked all the bedrooms but couldn't find anything out of the ordinary. The Rayado place had a large two-story main house with two large one-story wings going out at slight angles on the south side, one from the southwest corner of the main house and one on the southeast corner. This formed a courtyard between the two wings on the south side, and there was also a large portico on that side. The house had been built many years before by one of the previous ranch owners, and that entire family had died in the house many years ago. Local gossip claimed that the house was haunted because of many unexplained incidents that happened to more recent occupants. Of course Doug and Rita had no way of knowing this, but they would eventually find out more about it from personal experience.

Harlan received a call from deputy Frank Lucero in Las Animas county informing him that they were prepared to bring Spider in for questioning. Harlan told Frank that he would be there to help in any way he could. Early the next morning found him in Trinidad where a whole bevy of deputies descended on the Trujillo house. Some of the deputies covered the back of the property from a neighbor's yard. The side yards and front were all covered. Frank got on the bullhorn and asked all of them to come out. The first sign of activity was Anita, still in her pajamas, coming out the front door onto the porch.

"What the hell is going on?" she demanded.

"We need to speak to your brothers. Ask them to come out," Frank answered.

"My father is in there in a wheelchair. Please don't start shooting," Anita pleaded.

"Tell your brothers to come out and all will be fine," Frank insisted.

Anita went back into the house and her voice could be heard yelling at someone inside.

"Please don't start shooting. I'm bringing my father out," Anita yelled from the front door.

In a minute she appeared pushing a wheelchair. The old man looked to be partially paralyzed and somewhat distressed. His head lolled to one side and he was trying to say something, but the only sound was a moaning and crying noise. When she got the wheelchair to the top of a makeshift ramp beside the steps she said,

"I'm going to need some help here. I can't get him down the ramp by myself."

"I'll go help her," Harlan said, holstering his weapon and moving toward the house.

"Wait," Frank ordered, "This is not a safe situation."

Harlan didn't respond, but continued to the porch. "Hi, Anita. I'm sorry this had to work out this way. All we want is to talk to your brothers."

"I might have known you would be involved with this. Why are you harassing them?" Anita asked with her black eyes flashing angrily.

"Let me help you," Harlan said getting in front of the wheelchair.

With Anita in back they managed to get it down and behind a sheriff's vehicle when suddenly there was the sound of gunfire from the backyard of the house.

"Those stupid assholes," Anita screamed, trying to run toward the house only to be stopped by Harlan.

"Anita, stay here with your father. We will take care of this," he said reassuringly.

"Man down," the radio in Frank's hand blared. "Shots fired in the backyard...one perp is down and one deputy appears to be hit...we request an ambulance ASAP."

"Oh my God," Frank said more to himself than anyone else. "Control, requesting an ambulance at the Trujillo place. We have shots fired and there are injuries."

The two younger Trujillo brothers came out the front door with their hands in the air and begged the deputies not to shoot.

"Is there anyone else in the house? Where is your older brother?" Frank asked them.

"He's in the backyard. He's been shot. There is no one else in the house," one of the brothers blurted.

"Is that true?" Frank asked Anita. She answered by nodding her head, obviously shaken.

Frank ordered the deputies to search the house, while Harlan rushed around to the backyard, trying to avoid the fierce dogs that were tied around the premises. He found Spider sprawled on the ground near the back door with a gunshot wound in his chest. He then went to the back fence and grabbed the top rail to pull himself up. He peered over to see a female deputy lying on the ground with two other deputies tending to her.

"How is she?" he asked.

"She'll be fine. The slug went through the fence and hit her bulletproof vest. It knocked the wind out of her and drove her backwards, but I think she'll be okay," one of the deputies answered.

Harlan went back to Spider just as a couple of EMTs arrived and began treating him.

"Is he going to make it?" Harlan asked.

"He's been shot through one lung, so we are going to get him to the emergency room," one of the EMTs said.

"There is a wounded deputy on the other side of that fence who needs some attention, too," Harlan advised.

"I'll see to it," one of the EMTs said, grabbing his kit and hurrying off to the other yard.

"This didn't exactly turn out as we intended," Frank said, coming into the backyard.

"If I had known it would go like this, I wouldn't have asked," Harlan stated sadly.

"You win some, you lose some. We are going to search the house, get a forensic team in there, charge the younger brothers with something, and probably put them on probation. I think Anita can handle them without the influence of Spider."

"Yeah, she seems to try very hard at keeping the family together, but Spider is a disruptive influence," Harlan added. "Is your deputy going to be all right?"

"She's going to have one hell of a bruise, but thank God for bulletproof vests. She yelled at Spider when he came out the back door to drop his weapon. Evidently she fired at him the moment he raised his gun to shoot at her," Frank answered.

"Something else is going on here. I only wanted to question him about taking a phone call at the bar, but he acted very guilty. I wonder what else he has done?" Harlan mused half to himself.

After everything was mopped up at the scene, Harlan went to the hospital to see if there was any chance he could speak to Spider. He was shocked to find out that Spider had died on the operating table. Apparently the aorta had been nicked by the bullet and he bled to death internally. Harlan left the hospital feeling very dejected and very tired. He went to the sheriff's office and told Frank the news.

"May we interview the two younger brothers? It's possible that they know something?" he asked.

"Yeah, let's talk to them. Maybe they can shed some light on this whole mess," Frank agreed.

When the brothers were brought into the interrogation room, they sat across the table from Frank and Harlan.

"What are your names? I've never heard your names," Harlan asked.

"Mine is James," one of the young men answered nervously.

"I'm Jesús," said the other.

"James, Jesús, why did Spider do what he did today? All we wanted was to ask him some questions?" Frank asked.

James answered, "I don't know. He was asleep when he heard your bullhorn this morning. He was scared and started running around and looking out windows. Anita was screaming at us like it was all our fault. He grabbed his Glock and ran out the back door. Are Anita and Papa okay?"

"Yeah, they are fine, but I regret to inform you that Spider died in the hospital. I'm sorry," Harlan said.

Jesús took a deep breath, almost as if he was relieved, Harlan thought. He wondered how much these young lads were being controlled and manipulated by their older brother. James hung his head and started crying.

"What's going to happen to us?" Jesús asked.

"That depends on you," Frank stated. "If you cooperate I think I can talk the judge into giving you probation, but if you don't cooperate you're looking at jail time."

"What do you want to know?" James said looking up.

"Did Spider go to New Mexico about ten days ago?" Harlan asked.

"No, we all rode our bikes up to the Springs around that time, but not to New Mexico. We've been close to home since then," James said.

"What did you do in Colorado Springs?"

"Spider went to see some friends of his at a wrecking yard, and then we headed home."

"What did he do when he went to see these friends?" Frank asked, his interest suddenly peaked.

"I don't know," James answered.

"He gave them some money, a lot of money, and they gave him a big bundle," Jesús answered exchanging looks with his brother.

"What was in the bundle?"

"We don't know."

"Where is it now?"

"In the attic at the house," Jesús said.

"No wonder Spider was so nervous this morning," Frank stated.

"When you were going to or from Colorado Springs, did you stop at Bruiser's Bar in Walsenburg?" Harlan asked.

"Yeah, we usually do." James answered.

"Did Spider talk on the phone to anyone while you were in the bar?" Harlan asked.

"Yeah, Candice was talking to Nora and then she handed the phone to Spider. He talked to her a while and then went to give a message from Nora to Bruiser," James answered.

"Do you know what that message was?"

"No, he never said. We left shortly after that and came straight home so Spider could stash his stuff."

"Thank you for being honest with me," Harlan said as he

shook hands with both of them.

"It will probably be best if you guys stay the night here, and I'll try to get you in front of a judge tomorrow morning," Frank advised the young men.

Harlan found out that the forensic team had recovered Spider's stash of illegal drugs. Frank was relieved that the "Trinidad Cartel" had been shut down.

After the forensic team and law enforcement officials had finished with the house, and Animal Control had removed all the dogs, Anita, her father, and the two young brothers were allowed to move back in to enjoy a much more peaceful lifestyle. The two young men got jobs, Anita had a good job, and with Papa's supplemental security income they were able to have a decent life despite the turmoil of their past.

Rita woke Doug in the middle of the night and said, "Doug it's time!" It took Doug a few seconds to understand what she meant.

"How far apart are the contractions?" he asked, trying to remain calm.

"About ten minutes, but since we are so far from the hospital I think we should go," she answered trying to be calm after seeing how Doug was reacting.

"Do you want to go to Springer or Raton?" Doug asked.

"I think we have time to get to Raton. My obstetrician is there and I feel comfortable with him," she answered.

The Springer hospital was about twenty-five miles from Rayado, whereas Raton was a good sixty-five miles away. Doug loaded Rita and her suitcase, which had been packed for days, into his pickup and they hauled ass for Raton. When they arrived about an hour later the contractions were less than five minutes apart. Shortly after getting her in a room, the nurses took her into the delivery suite. Doug was allowed to go with her, but he felt totally useless and began to pace.

"With as many baby calves as you have delivered, I should have let you do this at home," Rita exclaimed after a big contraction.

"I was never nervous delivering a calf, but this is totally different," Doug said clutching her hand.

The doctor came into the delivery room and checked Rita, declaring that it wouldn't be long now. Two hours later Rita was exhausted—and Doug was exhausted, worried, and fretting. After examining Rita, the doctor said, "Okay, one more big push and this baby will be born."

Things are rarely as easy as people try to make you think they are, but after another thirty minutes of struggle, a beautiful girl was born. Rita and Doug were ecstatic. They were in total awe at this miracle, for that's what a new baby is. There is nothing more beautiful in this world than witnessing the birth of one of your own babies. It's at that moment when you understand that miracles really do happen.

"What are we going to name her?" Doug asked, looking at the tiny hand that was clasped around one of his calloused fingers and would forever be clasped around his heart.

"Kate—she looks like a Kate to me," Rita said.

"I hope she grows up to be as beautiful as you," Kate's daddy proclaimed.

Harlan contacted his boss as soon as he could after returning to Huerfano County, and he made arrangements for a meeting to explain what had happened in

Trinidad.

"One of the brothers actually told you that Spider relayed a message from Nora Lackey to Bruiser the day they were in Bruiser's bar?" the sheriff asked.

"That's what he said, and I believe him. Bruiser is a lot more involved in this than he is letting on," Harlan said. "I think we need to talk to him again."

"First let me get a search warrant for his bar, his house, storage unit, or anything else he has," Ed Sisneros suggested.

With warrant in hand, Ed and Harlan went to Bruiser's bar. There were a couple of local barflies sitting there nursing their beers, and two bikers were sitting at a table. The sheriff approached the bar while Harlan moved across the room where he could keep an eye on everyone that was in the place.

"Bruiser, I've got a warrant to search your place, your house, your storage unit, and your other properties," Ed Sisneros explained.

"This is harassment. You can't do that," Bruiser squealed, as one of his hands moved slowly under the bar.

"I wouldn't do that if I were you," Harlan warned. His hand was pointing a nine millimeter Glock directly at Bruiser's chest.

Bruiser paled and decided to put both hands on top of the bar. At the same time all of the patrons in the place decided they needed to be somewhere else almost immediately. The sheriff advised Bruiser to move out from behind the bar and sit at a table where they could keep an eye on him. Harlan checked to see what Bruiser had been reaching for and found an automatic pistol with a large capacity magazine clipped to the bottom of the bar. Bruiser's hand must have been about two inches from the weapon when he was halted.

As the sheriff and Harlan joined Bruiser at the table, a call came in to the sheriff's radio. The search teams had found a large stash of drugs in the storage unit and a Jeep in his garage. In the house there was a pair of hiking boots that the forensic team thought would match the plaster casts taken at the scene where Nora Lackey had been killed.

"Why did you kill Nora?" the sheriff asked.

Bruiser took a deep breath, exhaling it all before saying, "She knew too much. She knew all about my little operation. She knew Spider and his biker gang were my mules. When Spider told me where she was, I thought it was too good of an opportunity to pass up. She wanted me to come and get her, but she had to die, don't you see?"

"How did you know where to find her?" Harlan asked.

"She told Spider to tell me. She said to go to Angel Fire, New Mexico. As soon as I entered the town I was to look for a gate on the left that had a yellow scarf tied to the post. I was supposed to follow the road to the top of the mountain where I would find another gate. After that I decided to walk in and surprise her."

"And did you surprise her?" Ed asked.

"Yeah, she didn't know I was there until I knocked on the door. When I told her who it was, she opened it and I popped her. I made sure she was dead and got the hell out of there. You know the rest," Bruiser explained resignedly.

Jerry "Bruiser" Whitford stood trial in Colfax County,

New Mexico, for first degree murder. He was found guilty and transferred to death row at the State Penitentiary in Santa Fe. Some time later Harlan was talking with Celeste when he remarked,

"I can't believe this case is finally over. Remind me to call Doug and let him know how it ended."

"We could take a drive over there this weekend and see the new baby. Rita also has some ghosts she wants me to meet," Celeste said.

"Ghosts?"

"Yeah, but not to worry, they're friendly."

The following weekend they were all gathered around Rita's kitchen table discussing the events of the past year. The Martinez kids were playing in the courtyard, Kate was snoozing on her mama's lap, and all the adults had a cup of cowboy coffee.

"So why was it so important for this Bruiser guy to kill Nora Lackey?" Doug asked.

"He felt threatened because she knew too much. She worked for him for over ten years and knew all the in's and out's of his shady dealings. He had established quite a network of drug mules and pushers. There were some people who had a wrecking yard in Colorado Springs, which was a front for their illegal activities, and Spider and his gang transported their products around the area," Harlan explained.

"You know we are appalled by drug pushers and the whole drug culture, but do you realize that if no one used illicit drugs there would be no drug culture. The illegal drug market is just another case of supply and demand," Rita offered.

"Well said. But my guess is that we'd be shocked if we knew who all was using," Celeste said.

"So what's the answer? How do we fix it?" Doug asked.

"It has to start with good educational programs as early as elementary school. People have to be taught the damage drugs can do to our bodies and to families," Celeste suggested.

"I think a lot of it has to do with money. Politicians could put a lot more emphasis on stopping the trafficking if they really wanted to," Harlan offered.

"I wouldn't bet on that happening anytime soon. There's too much money involved, and likely some of them are users, too," Doug opined.

"You don't know that—you shouldn't judge," Rita scolded Doug.

"You're right—so how did Bruiser know where to find Garcia cow camp?" Doug asked, changing the subject.

"The yellow scarf. Nora tied it on the gate there at Angel Fire so he would know which road to take to the cabin," Harlan explained.

"So a yellow scarf led to her death," Celeste reflected.

"Bruiser's whole operation is crumbling. We passed our information to other law enforcement agencies and I've heard a lot of arrests have been made," said Harlan. "And just think—it all started with you finding a dead body and thinking it was a grizzly kill," Harlan marveled.

"Yeah, that's what it looked like to me at the time," Doug remarked. "But some good came out of all this, too. I met and married one of the most beautiful women in the world, and now we have a gorgeous baby girl," Doug said, grinning from ear to ear.

BC yipped from his rug by the stove. "Ah, yes, thanks for your help, BC. We couldn't have done it without you!"